The
Spirit of Laughter

Jonathan R. Rose

First Montag Press E-Book and Paperback Original Edition June 2020

Montag Press
ISBN: 978-1-940233-74-1
Cover design © Punto Ágora
Author photo © Alejandro Avendaño
Interior design by Niall Gray
Managing Director & Editor – Charlie Franco

A Montag Press Book
www.montagpress.com
Montag Press
1066 47th Ave. Unit #9
Oakland CA 94601 USA

Montag Press, the burning book with the hatchet cover, the skewed word mark and the portrayal of the long-suffering fireman mascot are trademarks of Montag Press.

Printed & Digitally Originated in the United States of America
10 9 8 7 6 5 4 3 2 1

I have always believed that one of the best compliments one writer can offer to another writer is to say: 'I wish I would have written that book'.

I know more than one writer, myself included, who will now owe that compliment to writer Jonathan Rose for his wonderful book, *The Spirit of Laughter*. He brings to his writing a unique and original voice that must be heard. Francisco Roberto Morelos, a fifteen-year-old artist, is the hero we are drawn to be. The one who, through laughter, courage and his artistic vision chooses to defy the authoritarian rule of those around him at school. Evil lives in many forms, but it is honor and love that will forever prevail. This is always the one thing that those who choose to abuse power will never truly come to understand. The artist's paintbrush, like the writer's pen, will remain mightier than the sword. It is from Francisco the artist, and Mr. Rose the writer, that we will forever be grateful for reminding us all of the fact that there are those who have the courage to do so every day of their lives. This is how rebellions rise and empires fall

— Gary Petras: author of *Memories End*, *The Sisters Hood and the Thorndancer*, *Small Heroes*, and *Farrow and Blackstorm* Trilogies

A powerful and carefully crafted novel about the possibility of growth—and rebellion—within the confines of an authoritarian system. Rose's protagonist, 15-year-old problem student Francisco, shows how an individual suffering under the reign of a corrupt and abusive principal can rely on art to find his own voice and express himself for the benefit of his peers. *The Spirit of Laughter* is a valuable antidote during this time when so many of our leaders are making toxic decisions.

— David Massengill, author of *The Skin That Fits* and *Red Swarm*

Jonathan R. Rose has crafted a story which is both compelling in its authenticity and attention to detail as well as bleakly humorous in an uncommon and wise way. The Spirit of Laughter promises comedy, and delivers this alongside a healthy dose of shared humanity.

— Nicholas Morine, author of *Kowloon Walled City*, 1984

This book is dedicated to the 43 Ayotzinapa students in Iguala, Guerrero and the 49 kids at the ABC school in Hermosillo, Sonora, and the countless other people in Mexico and around the world who have been taken by Evil.

1.

With his hands clasped comfortably behind his head, Francisco leaned back in his chair until its front feet rose from the floor. The teacher at the front of the class, Ms. Vasquez, recited words from a tattered history textbook. With a thud, the feet of Francisco's chair slammed down.

"Who cares about what happened a hundred years ago?" he said.

Ms. Vasquez stopped reading.

"I'm getting sick and tired of having to tell you this every single day, Francisco, stop interrupting."

He leaned back again.

"But there's only three weeks left of school, why are you wasting our time?"

The teacher, refusing to respond, carried on with her lesson. Francisco stared up at the ceiling, his eyes drawn to a long rod of flickering light hidden behind a sheet of cracked plastic. The light fixture looked like it was going to crash down on the unsuspecting student seated beneath it at any moment. Luckily for Francisco that student was not him. Instead, it was a quiet boy with a handsome face whose name he didn't care enough about to remember. After imagining the large piece of plastic slamming down on the head of the unaware student, he burst out laughing.

"That's it," Ms. Vasquez said. "I'm sick of your outbursts, Francisco. Go to Ms. Espinosa's office. I swear you must love it there seeing how many times I have to send you there."

"Not really," he replied, "It's just as boring there as it is here."

Laughter erupted from his peers. Francisco stood, smiled and stared at the unimpressed teacher who replied with a scowl. He picked up the knapsack resting beside him, walked out of the classroom, slammed the door behind him and walked down the school's main hallway toward the principal's office.

When he entered the office the secretary shifted her gaze from her computer screen, shook her head and said, "I see you've decided to join us again, Francisco. Ms. Espinosa is busy right now, so you'll have to sit and wait until she's ready to see you."

"Sit where?" he said.

"On that chair," she replied, "right beside you."

"But--"

"*Sit.*"

He glanced at the chair. It was old and rickety. He pressed his hand against it and heard it creak and crack, "This chair is going to break if I sit on it," he said.

The secretary tore her eyes away from the computer screen and glared at him.

"Just sit down, be quiet and wait for Ms. Espinosa."

"I would, but this chair is going to break, and I don't want to be sitting in it when it does."

The secretary groaned, stood, walked around her desk and approached him, "Listen," she said, "my job is to keep things running smoothly for Ms. Espinosa, not to take care of you."

Francisco looked at the secretary, glanced back at the brittle chair, then looked back at the secretary, "But the chair is going to break," he said. "Look at it. How can you not see that?"

"The chair is not going to break, Francisco. Just sit down and *be quiet*."

He smirked, and said, "So you *don't* think the chair is going to break?"

"*No*," the secretary replied. "It's not going to break."

He turned to the chair, placed his knapsack on it and watched it collapse. He looked back at the secretary.

"Do you still think it's not going to break?"

"Just stand and wait then," she replied.

He removed his knapsack from the pile of debris, leaned against a wall, crossed his arms and said, "I told you it was going to break."

Without responding, the secretary turned her back, returned to her desk, sat, stared at the computer screen and continued typing furiously.

Francisco's eyes wandered. He started making whatever annoying sound he could muster with his mouth. The secretary looked up and shook her head. Noticing how easy it was to irritate her, he increased the volume of his annoying noises, smacking his lips together.

"For God's sake," the secretary said, "you just have to wait a few minutes, Francisco. Why do you always have to cause trouble?"

"Because this is a waste of time, and the only reason I was sent here was because I told Ms. Vasquez what she was teaching was a waste of time, too."

"And was it a waste of time?" The secretary replied. "Why? Because you couldn't understand what she was teaching?"

The secretary flashed a condescending smile, and added, "Maybe if you *paid* attention instead of *stealing* it you would understand—"

"I understood *everything* Ms. Vasquez was teaching," Francisco interrupted. "It's history class. It's not like anything she tells us is going to change. Plus, there is only three weeks left of school and all I care about is my summer vacation, not some revolution that happened before my grandparents were born."

"Just because it's easy for you, doesn't mean it's easy for the other kids in your class," The secretary said.

"So?" he replied. "Why do I have to sit there bored out of my mind because *they* can't understand anything? Why do I have to be punished because *they're* stupid?"

He turned away from the secretary and searched the office for something else to occupy his attention, when he spotted a familiar portrait of the principal resting on a wooden mantle.

"Do you have a blank piece of paper?" he asked. "And a pencil, and some markers? I want to draw something."

The secretary shuffled through some papers and held up a single blank sheet along with a pencil that was half the size of a regular one.

"I don't have any markers," she said.

With the sheet of paper held in one hand, and the pint-size pencil held in the other, Francisco sat on the floor in a corner of the office beside the rubble of the collapsed chair and started to draw. The outline was completed quickly. He pressed, dabbed, tilted, rubbed and scratched the pencil's exhausted tip against the paper, utilizing whatever methods he could to add detail to the emerging sketch until his drawing started to mimic the image in his mind.

"Are you sure you don't have any markers?" he asked.

Without removing her eyes from the computer screen, the secretary said no.

He looked up to the sound of the principal's office door opening. There she was, Ms. Espinosa, the all-powerful ruler of the school. She looked down at him. Behind the principal was a man. Tall, prim and proper, adorned in a flawless black suit and red tie, the man looked down at Francisco and smiled, revealing a set of gleaming pearl white teeth. Francisco had seen the man's face many times in many places, yet couldn't recall the exact time or location, as if he were everywhere and nowhere.

"Hello son," the man said.

"You're not my father," Francisco replied.

Ms. Espinosa scowled.

Francisco recalled where he recognized the man from.

"He's the man from the billboards," he said. "My mom almost crashed the car on the highway because they distracted her. There were so many of them with him smiling down on everyone."

The man laughed.

"Why are you laughing?" Francisco said. "We almost died because of your smiling face. Are you a psycho or something?"

"*Francisco*," Ms. Espinosa said. "Get in my office and sit down."

Francisco made his way around the diminutive principal and the man whose face nearly killed him and his mother, and approached the door of Ms. Espinosa's office.

"Wait," he said, stopping mid-stride. "My drawing, I left it on the floor."

"Don't worry about your drawing," the principal said. "Just get in my office, sit down and be quiet."

Francisco was prepared to battle for the completed sketch before the man took a step, bent down, picked it up and glanced at it.

"How old are you, son?"

"I'm fifteen," Francisco replied.

The man handed the paper to Ms. Espinosa, while trying to subdue his laughter. The principal looked at the drawing before shooting Francisco an angry look. She turned the paper toward Francisco, showing him the picture he drew. It was a portrait of a ghastly face that resembled the principal's face on the portrait next to the clock, but with some important differences. The smooth, rich maroon hair from her portrait was reduced to a disheveled heap of grey strands. Her portrait's warm smile was replaced by a malevolent scowl and the flawlessness of the make-up covering the portrait's face was stripped away, leaving a severely aged, haggard face plagued with wrinkles so deep they looked like scars.

Ms. Espinosa's face glowed red with rage, while the man's was pink with pleasure. The man, unable to restrain himself, started to laugh. Francisco, deciding it best to follow the lead of the person he believed wielded the most power in the room, laughed right along with him.

"*Francisco,*" Ms. Espinosa shouted. "Get in my office, *now.*"

"You should listen to her," the man said.

"I'm so sorry," Ms. Espinosa said, turning to the man. "Sometimes these students are difficult to control, but you don't get awarded the number one rated school in the city five years in a row without learning how to keep the disobedient students in check."

The man nodded, "I have to go, but just keep doing what you're doing Edna and you'll be a shoo-in for a number one rating for a sixth straight year."

After the man left the office, Ms. Espinosa turned around. Her smile vanished. She stabbed Francisco with her eyes and told him to follow her to her office. Picking up his knapsack, Francisco watched the principal turn the office door's golden knob. It popped open. There was no lock, something he always found strange. She passed through the doorway, letting the door close behind her. He thrust his hand forward, catching the door just before it slammed shut. It was remarkably heavy. Once inside the office, the gentle caress of fresh, sweet smelling air, much different from the pungent aroma permeating throughout the rest of the school, welcomed him.

A series of framed photographs, shielded by thick plates of glass, adorned the office walls. All of the photos showed the principal either shaking hands with or half-hugging different people, while smiling so wide Francisco believed if she smiled any wider the corners of her mouth would have wrapped around the back of her head. He recognized many of the people in the photos in the same fashion he recognized the prestigious looking man he encountered moments earlier: from giant billboards, banners and posters overwhelming the city's streets and highways. Hanging on one of the walls were five gleaming, golden plaques, all of which gloated in elegant cursive, the school's number one ranking throughout the city.

After two steps, Francisco glanced at a door in the far corner of the office.

"What's behind that do—"

"I didn't say you could talk," the principal interrupted.

A moment of silence passed with Ms. Espinosa and Francisco staring at each other. After the principal turned her back to him, the silence was broken. The sound of her high-heeled shoes tapping against the floor echoed throughout the chamber as she made her way to her throne: a large, plush, leather-bound chair. Ms. Espinosa sat, while Francisco stood in front of her enormous desk. Built with black marble, the desk looked like a slab of night sky with millions of stars scattered throughout. He peered down and stared at the desk's glassy black face, but it did not mirror him back, stealing his reflection. Waiting for his punishment to be handed down, along with the lecture that was as surely to follow as surely as he was going to ignore it, Francisco stood, still and quiet, but Ms. Espinosa only stared at him. He started to fidget.

"Stop fidgeting."

He rolled his eyes.

"Stop rolling your eyes."

He huffed.

"Stop breathing like that."

Paralyzed, he waited for what would come soon. Ms. Espinosa slammed the paper with the sketch Francisco drew on her desk. He shook at the sound, breaking him free of the icy stance he had been forced to uphold.

"What possessed you to draw this?" she said, *"And what possessed you to draw it outside my office, in front of him?"*

"I drew it because I was bored," he replied. "And I drew it outside your office because that's where I was. Maybe if you didn't make me wait as long as you did, I wouldn't have drawn it."

Ms. Espinosa's mouth gaped open. Her foul, festering breath struck Francisco in the face. He closed his mouth and held his breath. His lungs ached. His eyes bulged. His cheeks expanded. He couldn't see it, but knew his face would soon change color, if it hadn't already. He had seen it on television: first red then blue. He continued holding on, hoping the principal's mouth would shut, sparing him the putrid smell of her breath, but her mouth stayed open. Precious seconds ticked by. Sweet smelling air was everywhere, begging him to breathe it in, but he refused to succumb to its allure, knowing the principal's rotten breath would push it aside. His whole body tensed up. He was near the end. He was about to open his mouth and welcome the pollution, when Ms. Espinosa bellowed, "Why are you holding your breath?"

After completing her sentence, the principal's mouth closed, shielding him from the poison, granting him mercy, safety, freedom to breathe. Ms. Espinosa held up Francisco's drawing and studied it, "I never knew you had such talent," she said.

Francisco remained quiet, suspicious of her compliment. The principal placed the sketch back on her desk.

"I think I have come up with the perfect punishment for you," she said.

He dug his heels in, preparing for what was to come, "Today I had an important meeting about the perception of this school. It was proposed to me that it needs a facelift. Now, I've made it my duty to turn this school into the best in the city, and over the last five years I've done that. Unfortunately, I think as a result of my dedication and diligence in providing kids like you with the best education possible, I've put less attention into other areas of the school. That is where you come in."

She smiled, stretching her colossal mouth from side to side, creating the kind of sinister grin found on the face of a nightmarish clown.

"Your drawing has allowed me to solve two problems at once. My first problem was to figure out how to uplift the school's appearance. I originally planned to hire several artists to paint the inside of the school's surrounding wall, but the problem with that is I would have to go through the trouble of finding the artists, then I would have to negotiate a reasonable price for their services, which, of course, can be very taxing, and very expensive. And this, Francisco, leads me to my second problem, which is how to discipline a young man who refuses to show respect toward those he should be respecting the most."

Francisco's face was a blank, bored slate. He didn't care about Ms. Espinosa's first problem, let alone her second one. His mind wandered and frolicked through a thick forest of thoughts that took him so far away that his eyelids sank and a dreamy smile spread across his face.

"Are you listening to me, Francisco?"

"No."

Ms. Espinosa sat back in her throne, "Are you comfortable standing here, in front of my desk?" she said.

"No."

"You have two choices, Francisco, you can give me your full, undivided attention, or you can stand right where you are for the rest of the day, which, according to my watch, is going to last for another five hours. Which is it going to be?"

He glanced at the golden timepiece wrapped around the principal's wrist, took a deep breath, and nodded.

"Good," she said. "For your punishment, you're going to paint the school's surrounding wall."

He groaned.

"Does this punishment upset you, Francisco? I have no idea why, since you seem to enjoy creating works of art so much."

Ms. Espinosa held up the sketch. With the drawing so close to her face, Francisco couldn't help but feel proud at how similar the portrait he drew was to the subject that inspired it.

"Since your specialty appears to be portraits, I want you to paint full body portraits of all your classmates. I believe it would be an excellent presentation of our school's spirit. Wouldn't you agree?"

"I—"

"Oh, and Francisco," she said. "You have until the end of the school year to finish the portraits."

"But that's only three weeks away."

"You're right," she said, after placing the sketched portrait face up, flat on her desk. "Since you have so much time, and there is a lot of space to cover, I think you'll have to paint portraits of not only every student in your class, but every student in your grade."

"But there must be over a hundred kids in my grade."

The principal opened a drawer, pulled out several sheets of paper, flipped through them, settled on one, skimmed through it and said, "There are only ninety-three, but I think ninety-two should do it. There is no point in painting yourself."

"But I don't even know how to paint portraits."

"Then I suggest you learn because I expect them to be perfect."

"How much time per day am I going to be given to do it?"

"Oh no, I couldn't possibly dream of standing in the way of your education," she replied. "You'll be working on this project after school hours, on your own time."

"And what if I say no?"

Ms. Espinosa ran one of her long finger nails along the sketched face staring back at her.

"If you don't have all of the portraits done by the time I take the stage for my year end assembly, I'll be forced to expel you. I'm not sure if you're familiar with the rules I've written personally, but if I have to expel a student, all of the fees their parents have already paid for the following year are forfeited. Do you know what the word *forfeited* means, Francisco?"

"They'd kill me," he said.

"That would be a shame," she replied.

"You can't do that."

"Really?" she countered. "I'm the principal, Francisco. I can do anything I want."

He crossed his arms across his chest.

"That seems to solve my problems," she said. "I'll be able to take the money I would have used to hire people to paint the wall and put it where I feel it'd be better suited, while you get to learn a valuable lesson in respect."

Ms. Espinosa grabbed the portrait Francisco drew of her, crushed it within her palm until there was nothing left but a deformed ball, and dropped it into the empty garbage can beside her desk.

2.

Francisco woke up dark and early at the usual time of five-forty-five. He yawned. With the sun still in its slumber, he walked to the bathroom and showered. The warm water pelted his skin, soaking him, awakening his senses and brightening his mind. After getting dressed and eating breakfast, he walked outside and was welcomed by the morning's brisk air. His father was waiting for him in the car.

The drive to the school was short in length, but long in time. Stuck in traffic, the car crawled through the city's suffocating streets, constantly stopping and going. Paused at a red light, Francisco smiled at an elderly woman draped in a green and yellow uniform. She sold his father a newspaper. Francisco's smile disappeared when he caught a glimpse of the newspaper's front page, where the graphic depiction of a dead, dark-skinned woman was sprawled front and center.

Francisco glared through the window, watching the city and its inhabitants pass him by until he reached his school. When he exited the car, he waved goodbye to his father who waved back before driving away. As he approached the school, he realized that he had forgotten the lunch his mother made for him. He looked at the face of the black, digital watch wrapped around his left wrist and saw he had two minutes to spare before the school's seven o'clock start time. Realizing he was going to have to do without food for a large portion of the day, the thought of eating what they served in the cafeteria made him shutter, as he continued on toward the building.

He paused at the school's front gate and stared at the large grey wall that surrounded the building. It was an empty, soulless sheet of cement, the blank canvas he was ordered to fill with the detailed figures of students he had no interest in knowing, let alone muralizing. Above the wall were three rows of barbed wire, each one in line with the others. Francisco passed through the gate and walked by a fat security guard sitting inside a tiny office. The guard didn't acknowledge him, his attention focused on a small television screen positioned directly in front of him. Inside the school, Francisco looked around, students wearing identical uniforms rushed by him, fearful of missing the morning bell. Then the bell rang. The last of the students rushed into their classrooms. Francisco stood in the center of the empty corridor. Door after door after door lined the long hallway. From behind, he heard somebody call his name. He turned and saw a guard who was just as fat as the one manning the front gate.

"It's seven o'clock," the guard said in between bites of a chocolate bar.

"How can you be sure?" Francisco asked.

"Because the bell just went off," the guard replied.

As the guard got closer and closer, he got fatter and fatter.

"Yeah, but how we do know the clock in the school is right? How do we know the bell went off at exactly seven o'clock? What if the bell went off at six fifty-eight? That means I still have two minutes left."

The guard continued to get closer and fatter.

"Don't be wise about it. Now get to your class, Francisco."

"But there are so many doors, and they all look the same."

"It's one minute past seven, Francisco. Do you really want me to bring you to Ms. Espinosa's office already?"

"Or is it six fifty-nine?"

Before the guard could answer, Francisco chuckled and said, "I'm going, I'm going."

Francisco walked into his class, and just as he expected, all of the students in the room stared at him stupidly. It was art class, and the teacher, Mrs. Ochoa, smiled and welcomed him. He smiled back at the teacher and walked to a vacant desk at the back of the room, but before he could sit, the teacher asked, "Problem with reading time, Francisco?"

"No," he replied, "But who can be sure what time it is? I don't know about you, but I don't trust that little clock hanging on the wall."

He looked up at an all too familiar portrait of the principal resting on a wooden mantel beside the clock.

"Honestly, I don't trust anything on any wall in this place," he added.

The other students in the class laughed.

"Francisco, please sit down," the teacher said, failing in her effort to repress a smirk of her own.

Mrs. Ochoa was Francisco's favorite teacher. Always kind and encouraging, she showed him the most tolerance. Lacking the condescension of Ms. Vasquez's voice and the callousness of Ms. Espinosa's, Mrs. Ochoa's voice was a steady stream of positive encouragement, rarely raising or lowering, always calm and controlled.

As Francisco stared at his fingertips, the teacher drew several three-dimensional cubes on the chalkboard. Dreary and plain, each cube appeared isolated and pointless. His fingers tingled and twitched. He rubbed his hands together until he had warmed his palms, imagining his hands bursting in flames. With Mrs. Ochoa's lesson showing no signs of life, he moved his feet, shuffling them along the floor, sweeping up the dirt, grouping it together into a messy mound. He looked up at the chalkboard, seeing nothing but the uninspiring cubes, he leaned back in his chair and tilted it back. The chair creaked with every slow rock until he tilted it too far and it crashed to the floor, taking him with it. Everybody in the class looked at him and laughed, while Mrs. Ochoa stared at him with concern. He got up, picked up his chair, sat and stared at the teacher with pleading eyes. He wanted to pay attention, he really did, but he couldn't force his body to care about a collection of empty boxes.

"I'm sorry," he said, "but they're just stupid cubes."

Mrs. Ochoa smiled at him. It was not the response he anticipated. Intrigued, he watched the teacher draw a number of lines joining the cubes together. This created a staircase that appeared to leap off the chalkboard with such clarity that he believed he could scale it to the ceiling. Seeing this, the tingle in his fingertips extinguished, his feet were still, he secured his chair and sat with his posture upright.

"I see your mind has changed regarding the stupid cubes," Mrs. Ochoa said. "I know adding another dimension, another layer, to just one square isn't special. I know you've all seen that before, but adding several layers, to several squares, and combining them to create something entirely different, that is special."

From there Mrs. Ochoa taught the rest of her class without a single disturbance from Francisco, who sat in his seat, quiet, attentive, enthralled. After the bell rang, Francisco hopped out of his seat and made his way to the door. Before he could leave, Mrs. Ochoa asked him to stay behind.

"I heard about the project Ms. Espinosa has forced you to do."

"She says if I don't finish it, she'll expel me and keep next year's tuition. Whatever. I know she can't actually do that," he said with a laugh.

"You should take her seriously," Mrs. Ochoa said.

"What do you mean?" he replied. "How can she be allowed to just steal money from students and their families?"

Mrs. Ochoa pursed her lips before responding, "Let's not focus on what could happen if you don't finish those portraits, and let's focus on how you *can* finish them."

"I don't even know how to paint portraits. I told Ms. Espinosa that, but she didn't care. I know I can draw, and I've even painted before, but painting portraits is completely different. How am I supposed to learn how to paint ninety-two portraits in just three weeks?"

Mrs. Ochoa sat in her chair and asked Francisco to sit in a nearby desk.

"I don't even know where to get the paint," he said. "Ms. Espinosa never even told me that."

"She told me where you were going to get it from," the teacher replied.

"Where?"

"Here," a scowl wrapping the teacher's lips. "She is taking the paint away from my art class and giving it all to you, so she can save money." She took a breath. The scowl disappeared. "I want to help you with this project, Francisco."

"How?" he asked.

Mrs. Ochoa just smiled.

"I'm going to prepare you some notes, a crash course on how to paint the portraits, and I promise you that by the time you've finished reading them, you'll be able to paint your classmates so vividly, it'll be as if you've brought them to life."

3.

Francisco, sitting behind a vacant desk at the back of his math class, dropped his knapsack beside him, let out a deep breath and slouched. The teacher, Mr. Ignacio, was babbling in a relentless monotone, systematically following his curriculum with the excitement of a eulogy. Francisco's eyes wandered, but there was nothing inside the classroom to distract him. He felt like a prisoner marooned on an island, left for dead. Mr. Ignacio turned his back to the students and wrote a series of numbers on the chalkboard. The teacher then dissected those numbers, turning them into fractions, before turning those fractions into more fractions, while pontificating about their significance. Francisco looked around and saw that at least five other students in the room had already dozed off. Trapped in the stifling classroom, Francisco forced himself to endure the endless yammering of the teacher, who continued to shrink more and more numbers into smaller fractions.

Begging for his teacher to arrive at zero, the nerves beneath Francisco's gums seized at the sound of the teacher's chalk scraping against the board with every fraction line, number loop and point. Boredom sat on Francisco's shoulder and whispered in his ear. He reached into his knapsack, took out a notebook, tore out a sheet of paper, scrunched it up into a tight ball and tossed it at the back of Mr. Ignacio's head. Laughter erupted from several of his fellow classmates. Mr. Ignacio spun around, exposing his face. It was a plain, flat facade devoid of anything memorable. The laugher ceased.

"Who threw that?"

Francisco looked around the class and saw several sets of judgmental eyes staring back at him. Even the students who were fast asleep when the balled up piece of paper was thrown awoke to stare at him accusingly. He was just waiting for every single one of his peers to point at him and chant, "he did it, he did it, he did it."

Refusing to give his classmates the satisfaction of selling him out, Francisco stood and said, "Why are you wasting our time with stupid fractions? Seriously, the only people who care about fractions are math teachers paid to teach about fractions that nobody cares about. Why don't you teach us something we *do* care about?"

"Francisco, sit down and let me continue my lesson."

The teacher turned his back and grabbed a small, shabby eraser resting on the edge of the wooden railing just below the chalkboard. He slammed the eraser against the chalkboard and wiped away all the numbers, erasing them from existence. He then picked up another eraser and clapped the two of them together. The collisions created white dusty plumes. The teacher then wrote a brand new set of numbers that stretched from one side of the chalkboard to the other and proceeded to shrink them into fractions far more complex than the ones he had just erased.

Francisco remained standing. He was stuck on a point of no return. To sit was to surrender, but to stand just for the sake of standing was pointless and would do nothing but render him a withered figure of indecision. If he was going to stand, he had to stand for something. He turned, grabbed, and tore a second sheet of paper from his notebook, scrunched it up, turned back around and whipped it at the back of Mr. Ignacio's head. The act took less than three seconds, but the shock sweeping through the classroom lasted well over half-a-minute. The teacher turned around. Satisfaction lit up Francisco's eyes, while rage flared in Mr. Ignacio's.

The teacher charged at Francisco, grabbed him by his shirt collar, leaned toward him and spoke in a grave tone.

"Get out of my Goddamn class Francisco and go to Ms. Espinosa's office."

Mr. Ignacio stood straight and composed himself before walking to his desk, where he ripped a small piece of paper from a notepad. He wrote something on the paper. A second later, he folded the paper, walked back to Francisco, handed the paper to him and ordered him to give it to Ms. Espinosa. Francisco looked down at the note, certain it contained words written for the sole purpose of condemning him. He was about to open the note and read it before Mr. Ignacio said in the same severe tone, "Don't you dare read it, Francisco, and don't throw it out because I will be talking to Ms. Espinosa about this after class. Now, *get out*."

Francisco returned to his desk, closed his notebook, grabbed it, stuffed it in his knapsack and slung the bag over his shoulder. During the short journey from his desk to the door, he gazed at his peers and saw nothing but blank stares. He shook his head and walked out of the classroom. As soon as he heard the slamming of the door, he opened the note Mr. Ignacio wrote and read the denouncing words before shoving the note back into his pocket. Getting closer and closer to Ms. Espinosa's domain, Francisco felt a tickle in his throat that in seconds transformed into unmistakable thirst. He reached into his pockets hoping there was enough money inside to buy something to drink at the vending machine located steps away from the principal's office, but he felt nothing except for Mr. Ignacio's folded note.

He closed his eyes and imagined an oasis within the grey walls and mottled floors of the school, but he didn't envision palm trees, lush foliage and a refreshing spring hidden behind sweltering mounds of sand. All he saw, all he yearned for, was a water fountain, like the ones he saw in movies and television shows, but as quickly as he conjured the fantasy, he opened his eyes, laughed and rejected it. Just picturing a steel spout offering an endless stream of refreshing water inside the school, available whenever it was desired, to whomever desired it, free of charge, was too preposterous, too absurd, to even imagine.

With the dryness of his thirst spreading from his swollen tongue to his lips, he remembered how the secretary always kept a large bottle of soda on her desk. He quickened his pace toward the principal's office. All he could think about was the cold, refreshing bottle of soda awaiting him. As he got closer and closer to the office, all he could visualize was the bottle, the prize, the Holy Grail, while simultaneously planning how to steal it from the unsuspecting secretary. She was always busy. It shouldn't be difficult.

Once he entered the office, Francisco immediately searched for and found the bottle he desired, right there, on top of the secretary's desk, large and full. He smiled when he saw the secretary typing away on her computer. He smiled even wider after realizing the secretary had not even noticed him come in. He was about to reach for the bottle when the secretary suddenly looked up, sighed, ceased her typing and shook her head. His smile disappeared.

"I see you're back again, Francisco. That's two days in a row, are you trying to make a habit of it?"

"Maybe," he replied, his eyes focused entirely on the bottle of soda.

The secretary shook her head again and told him to sit down on a chair that looked every bit as unstable as the one he destroyed a day earlier. The secretary's head sank, her fingers pounding the keyboard.

Francisco approached the secretary's desk and rested his hands on it. The full bottle of soda was well within reach. All he had to do was spread out his fingers, wrap them around the bottle, open, lift and drink. It was so painfully simple. His fingers trembled. The dryness of his tongue intensified more in the last few seconds than it had in the last few minutes. Desperate to quench his thirst, he no longer just looked at the bottle, but stalked it, staring at it as if it was the last bottle of drinkable liquid on earth. He just needed to distract her. A brief moment would grant him all the time he needed.

He inhaled.

"Ms—"

He stopped himself. He didn't know her name.

He desperately searched the secretary's desk for a nameplate, similar to the large gold one sitting comfortably on Ms. Espinosa's desk, but there was none there. There was nothing to identify the secretary. She was nameless. He considered abandoning the mission, but after glancing at the bottle of soda again, he dismissed the notion. He had to get it. He had to quench his thirst.

With the secretary's gaze resting on his face, Francisco forced a smile. Satisfied his smirk was sufficient enough to continue, he said, "Ms, there was somebody outside looking for you. They said they needed to see you. They said it was very important."

He uttered his words rapidly, hoping a pretense of alarm would bring him closer to success. The secretary looked at him oddly. He held his breath. The secretary didn't respond right away. Torturous seconds ticked away.

"Why didn't they just come in here?" she asked.

Stung, but not yet defeated, all he needed was an answer, but his mind was devoid of anything close to a plausible response. He panicked. Everything was going so well, only to be destroyed by the secretary's unexpected inquiry.

In a final act of desperation, he jumped up and down, flailing his arms around, shouting, "They need you. They need you. *They need you*. Hurry. Run. Go. *Now*!"

The secretary stood from her chair, walked around the desk and rushed to the door. Francisco didn't even turn around. He didn't need to see her leave. He just needed to hear the door close behind her. Once he heard the door slam shut, he wrapped his fingers around the bottle. As he had hoped, it was wonderfully frigid. With his other hand, he clamped his thumb and index finger around the bottle's cap and twisted it until he heard a familiar hiss. He leaned his face toward the exposed spout and smelled the soda's sweet aroma. The palm of his hand was gloriously numbed by the bottle's chilled plastic skin. He raised the bottle. It was heavy, worth its weight in gold. He brought the spout close to his lips. He could hear the fizzing of the carbonated fluid. The sound was magnificent. One effortless tilt of the bottle, a simple flick of the wrist, and the lovely liquid would stream down his throat, soaking everything it touched, invigorating his body like a miracle elixir. He brought the spout close. He felt several small bubbles bursting, playfully splashing his lips, whipping his palate into frenzy.

He awaited the satisfaction of his prize, when he suddenly heard a wicked voice ordering him to put the bottle down. He closed his eyes, hoping it was a mistake, an auditory hallucination, but when he heard the order repeated, he knew there was no mistake. Deciding to forgo consequence, he continued on, much faster than before, desperately hoping to drink all he could. He felt a splash of soda soak his lips before the bottle was snatched away. A torrent of black droplets splashed on the floor. With crushed eyes, he looked down at the innocent victims needlessly sacrificed. When he looked back up, he saw Ms. Espinosa gripping the bottle firmly in her hand. A moment later, the secretary came in and told him there was nobody outside before shooting him an angry glare. Ms. Espinosa put the bottle back on the desk, turned and made her way to her office. Without being told, Francisco followed her. For the duration of the short journey, he stared at the bottle of soda, and in a final heartbreaking act, he watched the secretary grab it and take a mighty gulp. After Francisco licked and swallowed what little remnants of soda rested on his lips, he realized that in spite of all his best efforts, he was still thirsty. He entered Ms. Espinosa's office and was immediately ordered to sit down on one of the two chairs resting in front of the principal's enormous desk. He loosened and removed the knapsack from his back before placing it on the floor beside him.

"I see you've decided to come back and see me," the principal said.

"Why does everybody always say I've *decided* to do this, or I've *decided* to do that?" he replied. "I didn't *decide* anything. I was *ordered* to come here. If it was my decision where to go, I definitely wouldn't come here."

Unfazed by Francisco's comments, Ms. Espinosa leaned back in her throne.

"So," she said, "when can I expect you to get started on those portraits I ordered?"

Never, he thought.

"Soon," he said.

"Excellent," she replied. "Just make sure they're done by the last day of school, or else you know what happens."

Refusing to let the principal's words affect him, Francisco replied, "What if my parents don't want me to stay after school?"

Ms. Espinosa leaned forward. Francisco couldn't tell when the thick layer of make-up on her face ended and her actual skin began. "I think your parents would prefer you stayed in this school a little longer each day, than to not have you attend this school ever again. Wouldn't you agree?"

Without responding, Francisco continued to stand by his belief that Ms. Espinosa would not, could not, follow through with her threat, but the more he tried to hold on to that belief, the harder it was to ignore the doubts looming in the distance.

"That's what I thought," Ms. Espinosa said. "Now, why are you here today? And don't bother lying because you know I'll find out one or way or another."

Francisco pulled the note Mr. Ignacio wrote from his pocket and handed it to her.

"I'm sure you've already read it, right?"

He shrugged.

She read the note aloud.

"I can't tolerate this student anymore. He is constantly disruptive, and today he threw a clumped up ball of paper at my head, not once, but twice. I don't want him in my class, and I have no doubt other teachers don't want him in their classes either. He is intolerable, is incapable of showing respect, and has no interest in being educated."

Ms. Espinosa read the letter with little enthusiasm. After she was done, she looked at Francisco, who showed the same lack of interest.

"What do you think we need to do about this?"

He shrugged again.

"You're not going to get off that easy, Francisco. No, I want you to come up with a solution."

He turned away from the principal.

"Look at me when I'm talking to you."

He looked back at Ms. Espinosa.

"I'm waiting," she said.

"Why do I have to come up with a solution?" he said. "You're the principal. First you want me to paint portraits on the school's surrounding wall because you don't want to hire somebody to do it, and now you want me to figure out what to do about me getting kicked out of class. What do *you* actually do?"

Ms. Espinosa hopped off her throne, circled her desk and stood in front of Francisco. She rested her right hand on his shoulder. He could feel her long nails digging into his skin through the fabric of his uniform shirt. Her breath was rancid. Dismissing fear and refusing to relent to its grip, Francisco smiled. Ms. Espinosa stood straight and stared at her young adversary, expressing a brief, yet unmistakable flash of disgust at his smirk. Without speaking, Ms. Espinosa turned and returned to her throne.

"Since you can't come up with a solution, I feel I'm forced to. What other classes do you have today?"

"Gym," he replied, "and—"

"I hope you enjoy it," she interrupted, "because starting tomorrow, you will only report to each of your classes to get the work necessary, and then you will sit on a desk here, in my office, all day, every day. Unfortunately, that means gym will no longer be part of your curriculum, so now you can work on the portraits after school hours *and* during your old gym class."

Francisco sighed. Experience counts for a lot in battle, and Ms. Espinosa's poise was rooted in years of crushing the spirits of her students. He was ready to concede, but her onslaught continued.

"Francisco, can you pass me that bag on the left side of my desk. I don't want to get up."

He looked around, stalling, hoping the principal would rescind her ridiculous request, but she just stared at him, waiting. Francisco scowled while staring back at Ms. Espinosa, doing all he could to make sure she saw, and remembered, the scorn on his face. He got up from the chair, turned, approached the bag, bent down and picked it up. The bag was heavy. He stood back up, approached Ms. Espinosa's desk and placed the bag on it. The principal grabbed the bag, while Francisco just stood there fuming over the trivial task he was ordered to carry out by a malignant woman who ordered him to do it only because she could.

"Can I leave now?"

Waiting to be dismissed, Francisco watched the principal reach into her bag, pull out a bottle of soda and place it on her desk.

"I saw you try to steal the secretary's drink."

I guess the secretary really doesn't have a name, he thought.

"Were you thirsty?"

He nodded, not wanting to give her the satisfaction of a confession.

"Don't you have any money to buy yourself a soda?" she asked, smiling the entire time.

He didn't answer.

Ms. Espinosa wrapped her fingers around the torso of the bottle with one hand, grabbed the bottle's head with the fingers of the other, and rotated it three hundred and sixty degrees, breaking its neck. In a high-pitched scream, the freshness of the soda departed. Francisco took a deep breath in an attempt to inhale as much of the soda's enticing scent as he could.

"That's too bad," she said.

She raised the bottle and took a long, satisfying gulp, until it was completely empty, before placing it back on her desk.

"Now you can leave."

4.

Standing in front of his locker, Francisco spun the steel combination lock in contrary directions, the movements based entirely on memory. He didn't even glance at the lock until he heard the familiar click and pop. He opened the locker. A meter-and-a-half in height and less than forty centimeters in width, chipped and rusted, the locker looked like a prison cell on an endless prison block, surrounded by other cells that looked just like it. He leaned his body inside the locker, grabbed his gym uniform and the pair of running shoes resting on the floor, and stuffed them into his knapsack. The bell rang. He closed the locker's door with a slam, sealed it with his lock and walked away.

He entered the boys' change room. While he didn't love the gym class itself, he cherished the time he got to wear the mandatory gym class uniform. With a more breathable, forgiving fabric, the shirt and shorts were a far cry from the restrictions of his daily attire. The white running shoes he was allowed to wear were also much more comfortable than the stiff, black shoes he and every other student were ordered by Ms. Espinosa to not only wear, but keep freshly buffed and polished.

Once he got outside, Francisco stood and listened to his peers talk, jostle, joke and ramble about things he cared little about, allowing his mind to wander. Stepping away from the student collective, he looked around. They were surrounded by a field of pavement. The only signs of life on the dreary grey sheet were a few patches of grass that had miraculously found a way to bust through the pavement and grow near the school's surrounding wall.

A whistle screamed behind Francisco's back. He turned around. Facing him was the gym teacher, Mr. Torres. Wide, tall and bald, the man radiated intimidation.

"Okay," Mr. Torres said, "now that I finally have all of your attention, you're all going to start the class by giving me five laps around the school. *Go.*"

The teacher followed his words with another aggressive blowing of his puny whistle.

Like dogs following a command, the group of students started to run for the sole purpose of appeasing a teacher who did nothing but stand and watch. Francisco was the last to break his stillness before following his classmates along the track that ran adjacent to the school's surrounding wall.

It was clear after the first few meters that the usual band of overachievers were more than happy to sprint ahead of the rest of the group and race each other for the glamorous title of pleasing the teacher the most. Francisco was sure he could have ran just as fast as the front runners, but when he asked himself the simple question of why, he struggled to find a satisfying answer, so he ran at his own pace. As he started the second lap, he could not help staring at the wall following him as he ran, glaring back at him blankly. Completing his third lap, his knees started to ache, and his thirst returned like a nightmare he was being forced to relive. His pace slowed, but that only exasperated the problem, as it meant he would complete the five laps in an even slower time than if he maintained the pace that was already severely draining him.

Beads of sweat fell from his brow and rolled down his face. His chest heaved. His head throbbed. His fingers swelled. He licked his lips, but the gesture was agonizing as his tongue felt like sandpaper. In that moment, he came to believe that neither his tongue, nor lips would ever taste the sweet relief of moisture again. He lowered his head, but abruptly rose it when he saw a group of students take sips from their bottles of water. As they passed him, he reached out his hand like a street urchin begging for food, but nobody noticed. They all just ran by him, leaving him behind as if he wasn't even there. With only one lap to go, he felt like he was at the edge of a plank, urged on by the tip of a sword. He took a deep breath, and instantly regretted it, as it felt like the sword had been thrust into his chest. With half of the final lap left, he was beaten and broken. Every step was an insurmountable hurdle. There was no sweat falling from his forehead. Fearing he no longer had any moisture left in his body, he was ready to give up. He looked around and singled out one of the sparse patches of grass near the edges of the surrounding wall. The patch wasn't large, but appeared comfortable enough, a good place to die. He staggered toward it. He was almost there when he felt somebody grab his shoulder. He turned around, and despite his weary vision, he managed to make out a pretty face.

"Are you thirsty?"

Doing all he could to resist shouting *yes* while snatching the bottle from the girl's hand, Francisco nodded his head and extended his swollen palm. The girl smiled and placed the bottle in his grasp. Leery that Ms. Espinosa would sneak up and snatch the bottle from him, Francisco looked around.

"What's wrong?" the girl asked.

He ceased his searching and looked at her face.

"I know you," he said. "I've seen you in Ms. Vasquez's history class. You sit at the front. Veronika, right?"

"Yes," she said, "and you're Francisco."

Not wanting to stave glory a second longer, he raised the bottle and guzzled the water. After his thirst was extinguished, Francisco lowered the bottle and was mortified at its weightlessness. He had drunk the entire thing. He gasped. He shook the bottle and was only able to see a few drops swishing around its plastic bottom.

"I'm so sorry," he said.

Veronika laughed.

"It's okay," she replied. "I knew you were thirsty."

"How?"

"You looked like you were going to pass out near that patch of grass."

Trying to come up with a way to subdue the burning sensation scorching his cheeks, Francisco turned away and wiped his face with the back of his hand. It was a poor solution, but it was all he could come up with. When he turned back toward Veronika, he said, "I thought I brought some money with me, but I forgot it, along with my lunch, so I wasn't able to buy anything to drink."

"So what are you going to eat today?" she asked.

He didn't answer.

"I brought a big lunch today," she said. "I can share it with you, if you'd like?"

Temporarily denied the ability to speak, Francisco smiled as wide as his jawbone would allow. His eyes brightened when he realized all it took to have such a pretty girl offer to have lunch with him was a debilitating bout of dehydration.

"Sounds good," she said. "Why don't we finish up this last lap?"

"Okay," he responded.

Fearing he was destined to live out the rest of his days as a mute, Francisco was overjoyed at his ability to speak once again. Still holding the empty water bottle in his hand, he started to sprint, but immediately slowed then stopped when he realized Veronika was nowhere to be seen. He turned and saw her standing there, smiling back at him, clearly holding back laughter at his sudden burst of energy. She jogged toward him, her long, dark hair swaying from side to side. Embarrassed, he found himself unable to stop staring at her chest, as he could see her still-developing breasts bouncing up and down underneath her shirt with every stride. He wanted to look away, but was stuck in his position, brazenly gawking as she got closer and closer. He dropped the empty water bottle. After bending down to retrieve it, he looked up and saw Veronika standing in front of him with a smirk on her face.

"You know it's rude to stare, right?"

He looked around like a moron, unable to focus on anything. All he heard was silence, painful, horrible silence. He didn't care there was less than one lap to go, he wanted to run a thousand laps just so he could get as far away from shame and humiliation as he could.

"This is where you're supposed to say you're sorry," she said.

He couldn't identify a hint of malice in her voice, but still wasn't sure if she was upset with him or not. He looked around again, just as moronic as before, searching for a solution, until he realized the solution was right there, charitably offered by Veronika herself.

"I'm sorry," he said.

Francisco finished the final lap. Rejoining the rest of his classmates, he looked at the group and saw many of his peers leaning down, panting, begging for breath. Mr. Torres marched in front of the exhausted children. Standing in front of the students, he stared at them with eyes of stone.

"What is wrong with all of you?" he said, "Are you all tired after just five laps? You're lucky I don't make you run another five just for taking so long."

Every student looked up at the imposing teacher with horror. Francisco ignored the burly man, as his focus rested solely on Veronika. He stared at her until she noticed him. Once he got her attention, he smiled. She smiled back. He made his way closer to her. He was almost by her side when Mr. Torres said, "Okay, now we're going to exercise. Since all of you are clearly out of shape, I want everybody to give me twenty-five push-ups."

A loud groan erupted from the group of students. A moment later, everybody was flat on their stomachs. Mr. Torres counted them down from twenty-five.

Angry that his goal to stand beside Veronika was thwarted by the teacher's request to do pushups, Francisco sprang up just as Mr. Torres finished shouting the number five.

"What do you think you're doing, Francisco?" the teacher asked. "You have twenty more to go."

"I want to know why I'm doing push-ups." he said. "If you can give me an actual reason other than because you said so, then I will happily finish them, but if you can't, I'm not doing any more."

"How dare you—"

"How dare I what?" Francisco interrupted. "How dare I ask a teacher why he's making me do something I think is pointless?"

The teacher narrowed his eyes, revealing a pair of simmering slits.

"Do you all agree with Francisco?" Mr. Torres asked. "Do you all think what we're doing here is pointless?"

Nobody said a word. Francisco rolled his eyes in disgust.

"I guess everybody here disagrees with you," Mr. Torres said confidently.

"Just because everybody is silent doesn't mean they agree with you," Francisco said.

"Silence *is* agreement," The gym teacher said. "I will not have this discussion with you, Francisco. We're all doing push-ups because I *said* we're going to do push-ups, and that's it."

"Why are you saying *we're all* doing push-ups? No *we're all* not. *We are*, while you're just standing there, trying to come up with new ways to torture us."

The teacher approached Francisco, stepping over several students, all of whom remained on their stomachs, quietly watching. Once he reached Francisco, Mr. Torres looked down at the smaller student, who looked up at the larger teacher with equal ire.

"You're going to listen to what I tell you, Francisco, or you can leave this class."

"That's the best you got?" Francisco asked. "This is going to be my last day in this class anyway."

He glared into Mr. Torres' eyes. The man's heavy breathing pounded his forehead.

"I have an idea," Francisco said. "It's kind of crazy, but why don't you actually let us do something we'll actually enjoy, something that will actually be fun?"

Francisco smiled. Mr. Torres did not.

"You little—"

"Why are you always so angry?" Francisco interrupted. "Did your mother not hug you enough when you were a kid?"

The students, who were all still laying on their stomachs, started to laugh. Mr. Torres grunted furiously and turned toward them. The joyful noise was immediately snuffed out. He turned back toward Francisco, whose smile remained.

"So you want to do something you'll enjoy? You want to do something fun? Okay, I have a great idea for something fun, Francisco. Give me five more, no, *ten more* laps around the school. Is that fun enough for you?"

Francisco sunk his feet into the soft soles of his running shoes, securing his position.

"No," he replied. "That would only be fun for you, which I think is pretty weird, but it's not fun for me, and it's not fun for them."

The rest of the students finally abandoned their deathlike positions. Some of them sat and some of them stood, but they all stared at Francisco and Mr. Torres.

"I think you're wrong, Francisco," the teacher said. "I think they would enjoy watching you run another ten laps very much. I think that'd be great fun for them, so I suggest you get started."

Hints of triumph seeped into the man's words.

Francisco didn't move a muscle. His fingers were perfectly still, not a single twitch. His legs were limbs of rigor. His mouth was obstinate. His entire body was a sculpture of utter refusal. There was a loud shuffle from behind the teacher. Mr. Torres turned and saw what Francisco had already seen. The teacher took a dramatic step back as every single one of the other students, beginning with Veronika, turned around and showed him their backs.

"I guess nobody wants to see me run, but you," Francisco said.

Mr. Torres turned back and faced Francisco, whose eyes glowed with glory, while the teacher's eyes blazed with fury. Francisco stepped around the teacher and joined the rest of his classmates, who all glared at him with expressions of shock. He sought out Veronika and stood next to her. She smiled at him. He smiled back. Together, they walked toward the surrounding wall, separating themselves from the crowd.

"Why do you always have to cause trouble, Francisco?" she asked.

"It's fun," he said, "and nobody else seems interested in doing it."

"What do you expect?" she said. "There is only three weeks left of school. All everybody cares about is summer vacation."

"That's all I care about, too," he replied, "but that doesn't mean I can't enjoy the time between now and then."

She laughed. He blushed. He looked away and stared at his peers, who talked, jostled, joked and rambled about things he cared little about.

"I can't believe I have to paint every single one of them," he said.

"What do you mean?"

He turned around.

"Espinosa said I have to paint portraits of everybody in our grade."

"Why?"

"I drew a portrait of her. I thought it was good. She didn't."

Veronika chuckled and asked what it looked like.

"Her," he replied.

Veronika asked Francisco where he had to paint the portraits. He raised his arm and pointed at the surrounding wall.

"Are you going to do it?" she asked.

"I'm still not sure. She says if I don't, I'll be expelled and she'll keep the tuition my parents paid for next year. I know she can't actually do that, but—"

"Of course she can," Veronika interrupted.

"No she can't. Everybody thinks she can do all these horrible things. She's all talk, just like Mr. Torres."

The bell rang. Francisco and Veronika walked toward the change rooms, but stopped when they both noticed Mr. Torres gazing back at them with a crooked smile. The teacher made his way toward them, stopped and stood in front of them, impeding their progress.

"I just confirmed you were telling the truth, Francisco, that this is to be your last class with me."

Francisco nodded before glancing at Veronika, whose sudden expression of sadness filled him with joy. She was going to miss him.

"That's too bad," Mr. Torres said.

Not bothering to respond to the teacher, Francisco turned back toward Veronika and gestured with his head that they leave. He took a single step, when the teacher, whose crooked smile remained, said, "Veronika, there was something I wanted to discuss with you in my office, can you please stay behind. It won't take long."

"Okay," she said.

She turned to Francisco.

"Wait for me in the cafeteria during lunch."

Francisco nodded. Veronika smiled at him, turned her back and approached Mr. Torres. Once she was by the teacher's side, they both walked toward his office.

* * *

Filled with long, metal tables running parallel to each other, the cafeteria was an enormous, hollow auditorium that kept the children's voices hostage inside its enclosed, concrete walls. Francisco sat and looked down both sides of his table. He glared at the seated students, all of whom leaned toward bland plastic trays with identical white plates filled with mounds of pale rice, a cutlet of chicken soaked in muddy brown sauce and a roll stale enough to shatter teeth. He looked down at his watch. Half of the lunch hour had elapsed. With every breath, he inhaled the wretched odor wafting from the food being consumed all around him. He glanced at a tall, gangly student seated to his left, who didn't eat, but shoveled his food into his mouth. Even when Francisco was able to spot traces of blood in the center of the student's slab of chicken, the student didn't seem to care and continued stuffing chunk after chunk into his mouth, smacking his lips with every chew. The sound made Francisco grimace forcing him to look away.

With only a few moments before the end of the lunch period, he couldn't understand why Veronika still hadn't shown up. He wondered where she was, if something had happened to her, if she was all right, or if she needed help. He wondered if she had no intention on meeting him at all and was just being polite by offering him the invitation. He wondered if she was mad about him drinking her water, staring at her chest, standing so close to her and making such a scene. He sighed, but his drawn out exhale was devoured by the adolescent discussions taking place all around him. The bell rang, and his stomach groaned.

5.

Barely able to squeeze his body between the hard-bottomed chair and the flat, jagged-edged table, Francisco held his breath so he could slide into position. Every exhale was met with the edge of the table piercing his gut, there was no escape. The malevolent amalgamation of splintered wood and twisted metal seemed to have been constructed for the sole purpose of inflicting pain on the students.

"Do you like your new desk?" Ms. Espinosa asked. "It's the only desk and chair combination piece we have, and since space is so limited in my office, I thought it was the best option."

He looked around Ms. Espinosa's spacious chamber then glowered at the principal, who stood before him, smiling.

"Is there a problem, Francisco? Just yesterday you questioned what I do here, and I thought providing you with the desk you will be sitting in for the rest of the school year would be a satisfying answer to your question, wouldn't you agree?"

He attempted to shift his body in a quest for comfort, but every movement, regardless how slight, was torturous.

"Are you not comfortable?" Ms. Espinosa questioned.

Francisco's pain became a ball of agony growing in the pit of his stomach, confined, just as he was in the desk he was sentenced to occupy. With the desk flexing its muscles against his ineffective attempts at loosening its clinch, he reached a threshold he didn't want to consider, while Ms. Espinosa, no doubt waiting for him to proclaim his submission to the mighty desk, remained where she was, her smile well intact.

He continued trying to find a relieving position, but his body was weakening. Ms. Espinosa's smile grew. Her nose flared with anticipation. Francisco's senses were bombarded with compression. Spirited groans made way for exhausted grunts as shoots of pain flowed through him. *Not much longer*, he thought. It was the only idea he could freely conceptualize amidst the blinding agony, but when he realized Ms. Espinosa was more than likely thinking the same thing, his body revitalized. He shifted again, and this time he was rewarded with a divine cracking sound. With his muscles taut, his mind clear and his eyes focused on the principal who appeared so eager to celebrate her victory it would not have surprised him if drops of saliva slipped from the edges of her exposed teeth, Francisco summoned all of his strength and rose. The higher he went, the louder the desk's cracking sound grew, until, when his body was near its pinnacle, the crack turned into a pained shriek, and with a proud breath, Francisco's protruding stomach pushed the desk past its own threshold, causing it to collapse and fall to the ground in a heap. He looked down at the remains of the defeated, sadistic desk and kicked it. When he looked up, without saying anything, Ms. Espinosa turned her back and returned to her desk. She hopped onto her throne and glared at the smiling student with predatory eyes.

"I guess I'll need another desk," he said. "This one is broken."

Ms. Espinosa pointed at the door.

"Get out, go to Ms. Vasquez's class, get the work you need and get back here. There will be another desk waiting for you."

Francisco turned, picked up the knapsack sitting quietly in a corner of the office, slung it over his shoulder, wrapped his hand around the golden doorknob and was about to rotate it when Ms. Espinosa told him to wait. He turned.

"That desk was very expensive, Francisco, so I'll have a bill waiting for you when you come back, along with those pieces you'll have to clean up."

Argumentative words rose up Francisco's throat, but were stifled when Ms. Espinosa repeated her order for him to get out of her office.

When Francisco reached Ms. Vasquez's history class, he glanced through the small window at the top of the door. The teacher was talking, and the students were listening. He took a deep breath, turned the doorknob and entered the classroom. Once inside, Ms. Vasquez turned to him. Without saying a word, she picked up a withered textbook and handed it to him. He accepted the book and put it in his knapsack. Before he could say anything, Ms. Vasquez continued her lesson, acting as if he wasn't even there, as if he were nothing more than a forgotten memory. About to exit, Francisco looked at his peers, who all stared at him with curious eyes. He was about to make his way out of the class when he realized Veronika was not there. Since gym class the day before, he hadn't seen her. He made his way back to Ms. Espinosa's lair. Once inside the principal's office, he saw her talking on the phone.

"So if I let the guards go a week early, how much will I save?" she said.

"Ms. Espinosa, do you know what happened to Veronika?"

The principal cupped the bottom of the phone, shushed Francisco and continued her conversation.

"Sorry about that, no, no, nothing important, just a student. Anyway, so how much did you say... really? That's excellent. I'll definitely do that then... am I worried? No. Why?"

Francisco looked down and saw a desk and chair he was sure was for him. To his relief, it was not a combination piece like the unforgiving contraption he defeated less than thirty minutes ago. He put his knapsack down, pulled the chair out, sat down and put his arms on the desk, awaiting any kind of threatening action from it. He shifted his body in the chair, awaiting a cracking sound, but none came. He reached into his knapsack, pulled out the textbook he received from Ms. Vasquez and the notebook he used to tear out sheets of paper he threw at Mr. Ignacio, placed them on the desk and dropped his bag on the floor.

Satisfied the desk was not going to maim him, Francisco stood from the chair and said, "Ms. Espinosa, do you know what happened to Veronika?"

The principal stared at him, told whomever it was she was speaking to on the phone she would call them back, and hung up.

"What is the problem, Francisco? Do you not agree with the bill I left you?"

"What bill? I don't care about a bill, I care abo—"

"Good," Ms. Espinosa interrupted. "Then sit down and start your work."

Francisco remained standing and said, "I want to know what happened to Veronika. Is she missing?"

Ms. Espinosa looked at him quizzically.

"Who?"

"Veronika," he said. "She's in my grade. She has long, black hair."

"You mean Veronika Cardenas?"

Before Francisco could reply, Ms. Espinosa started to laugh. He looked around hoping to find something he could throw at the unconcerned educator's head.

"She's not missing Francisco."

He waited for an elaboration, but none came. Frustrated with the principal's withholding of information, he stepped toward her desk and leaned over it. She hopped off her throne and leaned back toward him.

"I want to know what happened to Veronika," he said.

"What happens to students in this school is not your concern Francisco, it is my concern, and my concern only."

Francisco straightened his body and replied, "Then why aren't you concerned about what happened to Veronika? She's a student isn't she?"

Ms. Espinosa sat back down on her throne. A breath exhaled from the plush leather.

"Francisco, your concern should only be focused on yourself."

"Veronika," he said, "what happened to her?"

Ms. Espinosa raised her hand and cupped her chin.

"I told you before, Francisco, it's not your concern."

Francisco leaned back toward the principal and placed both his palms on the desk's black, marble surface.

"Why won't you just tell me?" he questioned.

"Because I don't have to," she replied, her eyes boring into his. "You are a student and I am the principal. I'm in charge, not you."

Francisco took a deep breath and did something he thought he never would.

"Ms. Espinosa, can you *please* tell me what happened to Veronika?"

He swallowed, hard, believing vomit was going to follow his words as an encore. The nausea intensified when he saw Ms. Espinosa's hideous smile form and spread, stretching her face's overly made-up skin.

"I don't think I've ever heard you say please to me before," she said. "Say it again."

He took another deep breath and said, "*Please*, Ms. Espinosa, can you tell me what happened to Veronika?"

The principal leaned back in her throne. The creaking of the chair's spine along with the soft exhale of the chair's leather cushion combined to create a mocking cackle that Francisco believed was meant for him.

"She was suspended from school."

"For how long?" he asked.

"Today is Wednesday, right?"

Francisco nodded affirmatively. The principal began counting. She extended one finger after another, each one armed with a nail far exceeding the length of the tip, until only one finger stayed dormant.

"I suspended her yesterday, so she'll be back next Monday. Now sit down, and get to work."

"What did she do?"

"That's none of your concern."

"Just tell me."

"No."

Francisco sat. Trembling with frustration at the stonewalling, he shuffled the books in front of him and saw the bill Ms. Espinosa mentioned to him earlier. He gasped at the amount, but before he could speak, Ms. Espinosa said, "What's the problem now?"

"The bill," he said.

"What about it?" she replied.

"That's a lot for an old desk, isn't it?"

"You had your chance to discuss the bill, but you wanted to talk about Veronika and her suspension instead."

"But, it's so mu—"

"Either you give the bill to your parents today, or I call them right now and tell them the amount and why I'm charging it," she said. "It's your choice."

Refusing to concede a spoken word, Francisco crushed the bill in his hand and stuffed it in his pocket.

"Now get to work," the principal said.

He opened both his textbook and notebook. After reading a few words from the ratty textbook, he stared at a blank page from his notebook. He looked up at Ms. Espinosa. The principal's attention was on several things, the telephone in front of her, a set of papers on her desk, the celebratory photos on her wall, anything but Francisco, until he said, "What am I supposed to do?"

"You're supposed to work," she replied.

"I would love to," he lied, "but I have no idea what work I'm supposed to do."

"You should have found that out before leaving Ms. Vasquez's class," Ms. Espinosa replied.

"I would have," Francisco said, "but she didn't say a word to me."

"Maybe she would've told you what work you were supposed to do if you didn't keep causing trouble in her class."

"I wouldn't have caused trouble in her class if she actually *taught* something instead of repeating the same thing over and over again."

"She's a history teacher, Francisco, and that's how history works, it repeats itself, over and over again."

He slammed the textbook shut. The rest of the period went by in silence. When the bell rang, he pushed the desk forward, scraping the floor. He hoped the noise was loud enough to annoy the principal. He got up and grabbed his knapsack. He was about to dart out of the office before Ms. Espinosa reminded him not to forget to return the textbook to Ms. Vasquez. He didn't respond to Ms. Espinosa's order. He didn't even turn around to acknowledge it.

Once outside the office, he was met with a horde of students who rushed through the hallway, forcing him to bob and weave through the mass of youth. A few moments elapsed before the crowd dissolved and Francisco's mind suddenly cleared, making room for thoughts ruled by a single question: *why did Veronika get suspended?*

He made his way through the empty hallway to Ms. Vasquez's classroom, trying to unravel the mystery behind Veronika's absence in his mind. He knew Mr. Torres had to be involved because he was the last person that he saw be with Veronika before her suspension. He reached the door of Ms. Vasquez's classroom, but walked right by it. He passed classroom door after classroom door, his pace quickening. When he finally came to a stop, he looked forward. In front of him was a door he was sure would lead him to the answers he sought. He rotated the doorknob until the door popped open.

Now outside, he looked around, but nobody was there. Knowing Mr. Torres never came out of his office until all of his students were changed and standing together, awaiting his arrival, Francisco stood in the center of the school's field of pavement. The first boy came out of the change room, followed by a second, third, fourth and fifth. Girls streamed out from the other change room, one by one, all dressed in the same gym uniform Veronika wore. As all of the students came out, they started congregating in front of Francisco, staring at him awkwardly. He cleared his throat before loudly declaring he was waiting for Mr. Torres and wasn't going to leave until he spoke to him. A boy with a brutish face laughed.

"What's so funny?" Francisco questioned.

"You're going to be waiting for a long time," the boy replied.

"What are you talking about?"

"He ain't here," the boy said. "We got a supply."

The boy pointed beyond Francisco's back. Francisco tried to spin around, but slipped on a crack in the slab of pavement beneath his feet and fell to his knees. The boy and several other students standing beside and behind him laughed as Francisco fell crumpled onto the pavement.

"Who are you and what at are you doing there?"

Francisco looked up. Standing above him was a large man, similar in size to Mr. Torres, but appearing less authoritative, less combative and less mean. Francisco stood. He felt a shooting pain throbbing around his knees. He looked down. His pants were torn, exposing a pair of scraped kneecaps. Francisco looked the man in the eye and said, "I'm looking for Mr. Torres."

"He's not here."

"Do you know what happened to him?" Francisco asked.

"No," the man said. "All I know is I'm replacing him until Monday. I'm sorry, but what is your name?"

"My name is Francisco, Francisco Roberto Morelos."

"Well, Francisco, I was given strict instructions that if any student in this class comes without their proper gym uniform, I have to send them to the principal's office."

"You don't have to send me anywhere," Francisco said. "I'm going there anyway."

Before the supply teacher was able to respond, Francisco turned and made his way to the door leading him back into the school. Once he was inside the building, he made his way back to Ms. Espinosa's office. With the school's main hallway free of activity, Francisco ran, extending his strides to the fullest capacity of his legs. Imagining that he was getting closer to the answers he desired, he ran faster, ignoring the ache of his knees. The mystery was going to be solved. He ran even faster. The office came into view, when he was abruptly stopped by one of the school's two fat security guards.

"Where are you going so fast, Francisco? Why aren't you in class? And don't tell me the clocks are wrong again."

"I'm sure the clocks are fine," Francisco replied. "I have to go."

"You either get to class, or I'm going to take you to see Ms. Espinosa."

"Perfect," Francisco said.

"What?" The guard said.

"That's where I'm going. You don't even have to take me, just move out of the way and I'll go there myself."

The guard took a huge bite from a pastry he held in his hand. "I don't think so, Francisco," the guard said mid-chew. "I'm not going to fall for another one of your tricks."

"What tricks? You told me to either go to class or see Ms. Espinosa, I choose door number two."

The guard took a step back. Believing the guard backtracked as a gesture permitting him to pass, Francisco took two rapid strides toward the office before he felt the guard's doughy hand grab the back of his shoulder. Francisco spun around. "What are you doing?"

"I don't think so," The guard said. "I know the minute I walk away, you're going to wait in the washroom over there until I leave, and then you're going to go somewhere else. I'm not stupid, Francisco. *Nobody* in this school wants to see Ms. Espinosa."

Francisco's head sank. "Listen, I'm not playing any tricks on you. I'm telling you the truth. I want to see Ms. Espinosa."

The guard smiled. His grip around Francisco's shoulder tightened. "Sure you do," the guard said after taking yet another large bite of his pastry. "Listen, just tell me which class you have to go to and we can walk there together."

Francisco's entire body tensed up. He spun around once again, hoping to slither his way out of the guard's grip, but the guard held him as tight as he had held his pastry. Staring at the office door, Francisco quietly muttered the first alternative that came to mind, "Mrs. Ochoa's class, room 116."

"Perfect," the guard said. When they finally reached the door to Mrs. Ochoa's classroom, the guard relinquished his grasp, freeing Francisco. "Now, go to class." The guard walked away, indulging in the final bite of his pastry.

Francisco entered the classroom. There were no other students inside. Mrs. Ochoa stood from behind her desk. "Francisco," she said in her usual soft, soothing tone. "I was actually going to go looking for you. I've finished the notes I told you about."

Confused, Francisco asked her why nobody else was inside.

"I don't teach every period," she said. "There have been cutbacks to the art program because money needs to go where it's *better* suited." She shot an angry glance at the portrait of Ms. Espinosa resting on its mantle before opening a drawer in her desk. She reached into the drawer, pulled out and handed Francisco a well-nourished notebook. He accepted it half-heartedly, his mind still focused on the undetermined nature of Veronika's suspension. "This will help you bring those portraits you have to paint to life, just like we talked about."

He opened the book and flipped through the pages. It was filled with diagrams, explanations, points and scattered sentences. He believed it would take him at least a week to read the entire thing.

"Do you think Ms. Espinosa can *really* expel me and keep next year's tuition if I don't finish the portraits?" he asked.

Mrs. Ochoa looked around the room, glanced at the principal's portrait again, looked back at Francisco and said, "Hopefully it won't come to that."

Francisco thanked the teacher, made his way to the door, turned the knob and walked out of the classroom. Once again, he was in the school's empty main hallway, except this time he was on the other side of the school, far away from Ms. Espinosa and the answers he knew she possessed. Recalling the ineffectiveness of sprinting through the school, Francisco erred on the side of caution. He tightened the straps of his knapsack, eliminating all space between the bag and his back. His walk resembled a vertical crawl as he stealthily made his way through the building's main hallway. His eyes were two orbs of observation, surveying his surroundings with a feline-like vigilance. If anything within his line of sight moved, he was going to see it. If any noise was made, he was going to hear it. Maintaining his precise pace, Francisco continued down the school's throat, knowing it would lead him to the belly of the beast.

Up ahead, an unseen door opened then closed with a slam. He froze. He wasn't panicked at the sound, but ready for what could come as a result of it. He looked around. There was no cover, nowhere for him to hide. Knowing he could not remain standing in the open, where he was susceptible to capture, he darted to a nearby wall. He looked in every direction. There was nothing. It had to be the guard, returning for the sole purpose of denying his objective. He took a deep breath and reassessed his surroundings, trying to find a way to move forward, while not being seen. He spotted a garbage can. It was stuffed with trash ready to spill like a secret too difficult to keep. He rushed to the garbage can and knelt behind it. In a position of readiness, he was prepared to pounce at whoever was looking to impede his progress. He waited. His mind was clear, his breathing steady. His fingers tingled with anxiousness. Tension built up in his legs, stinging his sore kneecaps. He rose slowly from his hiding spot. With only his brow visible above the garbage can's squalid peak, he looked around and saw nothing. Just as another deep, slow, controlled breath came to its end, his left leg suddenly gave way, slightly, but enough to strike and disrupt the garbage can's fragile state, causing a number of crushed soda cans and crinkled candy wrappers to crash to the ground. The sound of their impact echoed throughout the corridor.

Left with no time to think, only to react, Francisco left his position and scurried to the other side of the hallway. He looked in both directions and saw nothing. He looked ahead, focusing his eyes as much as he could, hoping to gain just one more meter of clear vision, but still he saw nothing. He ran down the hallway. He passed door after door until he was once again within view of the school's main office. He stopped, leaned against a rusted locker that creaked in a devious attempt to expose him, held his breath and looked around, believing that despite the ridiculous odds of the same fat guard waiting for him there, it was best to be sure. Refusing to jeopardize his chance, he made his way to the nearby washroom that the guard had pointed at earlier.

He went into the washroom and closed the door enough to conceal his body, but not his vision. The odor from within the washroom was so rancid, so thick, he could taste it. Holding his breath, able to see outside the narrow crease between the door and its ragged frame, he stared at his desired destination. He waited thirty seconds before opening the door wider. He stepped out of the washroom and exhaled. He inhaled and looked to one side. There was nothing. He looked to the other side and saw nothing. He exhaled and made the final dash to the office.

He reached the office door and turned the doorknob. Once inside, he looked directly at the entrance to his answers. He walked toward it, ignoring the secretary, who returned the favor while madly typing away on her computer. Filled with nervousness at the unknown, he turned the golden handle, pushed the heavy door and walked in.

Ms. Espinosa was sitting on her throne, shifting through some papers, signing some and ignoring others. He pondered the power of her signature, the significance of each paper she signed and the fate of those she didn't. He walked toward her desk. She looked up.

"I see you're back to do more work," she said.

"What happened between Mr. Torres and Veronika?" he asked.

The principal stared at Francisco with a coolness that chilled the sweet smelling chamber.

"I told you before it's none of your concern. I suggest you let it go."

"I want to know what happened," he said. "Veronika gets suspended for almost two weeks, the longest suspension I've ever heard of, and Mr. Torres is away until Monday. *What happened?*"

Ms. Espinosa leaned back, the creaking sound of her throne prolonged. Waiting for a reply, Francisco loosened the straps of his knapsack, dropped it to the floor and crossed his arms across his chest. The principal leaned forward, her eyes shrewdly looking him up and down.

"Pass me the bill I gave you earlier," she said.

He reached into his pocket and pulled out the crinkled, exorbitant bill for the broken desk. He hesitated before handing it to her, trying to figure out the cunning woman's angle. "Why do you want it?"

"Pass it to me."

He did as he was told, for the sole purpose of seeing what was going to happen as a result. Ms. Espinosa took the bill and scribbled something on it. After she was done, she handed it back to Francisco. There was now a different amount written at the bottom of the paper.

"This is *double* what it was before."

"Yes it is," she said. "I noticed the large rips in your pants. My students must always be presented impeccably, and when they're not consequences must be paid. It's about perception Francisco, and perception has a price."

He looked down at the bill, shook his head and replied, "Yeah, and it's pretty damn high."

"Perception is reality, Francisco, and it must be maintained at all costs."

"But there is only a few weeks left of school, why do I need a second pair of pants?"

"I have to be fair, Francisco, if every student has to own two pairs of pants at all times, how could I, in good conscience, not enforce that rule on you?"

He bent down and investigated the rips in his pants. Though large, they were easily repairable.

"But why do I have to pay so much?" he asked. "My mom could just fix them."

"I'm sorry Francisco, but I can't trust the reputation of this school with your mother's stitching abilities. No, you'll have to buy another pair of pants."

"Can't I just buy a cheaper pair of pants on my own?"

Ms. Espinosa shook her head.

"No," she said, "you must buy the pants through the school."

He angrily stuffed the bill back into his pocket, grabbed his knapsack, opened it and emptied it on his desk. The large textbook he neglected to return to Ms. Vasquez slammed on the table with a brutal thud.

"Fine," he said. "I'll tell my parents they have to buy me new pants. Now can you tell me what happened between Veronika and Mr. Torres?"

Ms. Espinosa looked at Francisco's desk.

"Pass me the bill one more time."

"Why?"

"Pass me the bill one more time," she repeated.

He grabbed the bill in the depths of his pocket, pulled it out and slammed in on the principal's desk. Just as she did before, Ms. Espinosa scribbled on the paper and handed it back to him. His head tilted forward. The amount had increased yet again.

"Why did you add to it?"

Ms. Espinosa leaned forward and said, "You were supposed to return that textbook to Ms. Vasquez before the start of your next class, and since you didn't do as you were told I'm charging you a fine."

"I can take it to her right now," he said.

"That's not the point, Francisco, the point is—"

"You want more money," he interrupted.

Ms. Espinosa smiled.

"It's not about the money, Francisco, it's about being responsible for your actions."

He returned the bill to his pocket, stuffing it as deep as he could in hopes it would disappear in the pouch's fabric.

"Why won't you just tell me what happened between Veronika and Mr. Torres?" he questioned.

Ms. Espinosa gazed at him, not a hint of emotion was visible on her made-up face.

"It's your choice what you want to do, Francisco. You can keep asking me the same question and keep learning about responsibility, or you can forget about it, sit down and do your work."

Knowing that this arduous journey was at its end, he sat down at his desk. Ms. Espinosa returned to her stack of papers, signing some and ignoring others. He had to wait. He had no choice. The answers he wanted were only going to have to come from the mystery's source.

Francisco grabbed his knapsack, opened it, put the costly textbook back inside, pulled out the notebook Mrs. Ochoa gave him and opened it to the first page. From the moment he read the first word Mrs. Ochoa wrote for him, Francisco was engrossed. His eyes never left the notebook's pages until the bell rang. He devoured the book's words, voraciously scouring every line. On several occasions he re-read the same line multiple times, fearing he might have missed something. His concentration was so intense his hands started to sweat. His wet fingertips became acidic, corrupting the corners of each page, leaving a dampened stain that grew by the second, forcing him to read even faster.

Mrs. Ochoa's words were like sumptuous helpings for the starving, fresh water for the thirsty, hope for the bleak, love for the lonely. Her words, diagrams, tips and tactics, invigorated him. And while he knew she wrote and drew what she did in hopes of teaching Francisco to bring his portraits to life, they did much more than that. They brought *him* to life. She freed him from the suffocating clutches of a question he could not get answered. When the class bell rang, Francisco stood. Reluctantly he closed the notebook and put it in his knapsack. He was desperate to read more. He slung the knapsack over his shoulder and left the office.

He then walked into Ms. Vasquez's class, dropped the textbook on her desk and left. Not a single word was exchanged between him and the teacher. After leaving Ms. Vasquez's class, he made his way to Mr. Ignacio's math class. He entered and was met with a large, victorious smile on the teacher's face. He took a deep breath. He wanted to wipe Mr. Ignacio's smirk away, but the focus and energy required to do so were absent, prisoners of distraction. All he could think about was returning to his desk in Ms. Espinosa's office, so he could continue reading Mrs. Ochoa's magical words.

"I bet you regret throwing those pieces of paper at me now?" Mr. Ignacio said.

Francisco looked up at the teacher, but the man's face, once thought of as nothing more than a forgettable sheet, as blank as the paper he threw at his head, appeared drastically different. It was a yearning canvas, full of opportunity. The teacher continued talking about his victory, but all Francisco could see were ways he could transform and illuminate the older man's features using the tips and tactics he learned from Mrs. Ochoa's notebook. He recalled a method to make Mr. Ignacio's cheeks appear plump, to thicken his hair, to increase or decrease his age by manipulating the slender rings surrounding his eyes. He was even able to brighten the teacher's shoes with cleverly supplemented sheen. There were so many choices, so many options.

"Are you listening to me, Francisco?"

"No," Francisco replied.

He slung his knapsack over his shoulder, pulled out Mrs. Ochoa's notebook and disappeared right in front of the simmering math teacher, travelling millions of miles, venturing to a place where nothing and nobody was within reach, just him and the opened book held firmly in his grasp.

"*Francisco*," Mr. Ignacio said.

"What?" Francisco replied.

Appearing to realize the fruits of his victory were growing scarce, Mr. Ignacio tried to hand Francisco a large, heavy textbook and told him what questions to answer. Francisco refused to accept the paper filled brick, and without saying a word he walked out of the classroom and made his way to Ms. Espinosa's office.

He held up Mrs. Ochoa's notebook in front of his face for the duration of the journey, absorbing everything from its pages. When he reached the principal's office, he walked in, said nothing, sat in his desk and continued reading. He was halfway through the notes he had thought would take him at least a week to finish when he heard the bell ring. It was a marvelous sound. He jumped out of his desk, looked at the principal who showed no interest in his presence and said, "I think I'm ready to start in on the portraits."

Staring at several sheets of paper spread out before her, without looking up, the principal replied, "Just make sure those portraits are perfect, and are done before the last day of school, or else you know what happens."

6.

Francisco rushed out of the principal's office and ran through the school's main hallway. When he reached Mrs. Ochoa's classroom, he whipped the door open, walked in, saw the teacher sitting quietly and said, "I'm ready to start."

Mrs. Ochoa looked up at him and smiled.

"I'm glad to hear it," she said, "You've already finished reading all of the notes I prepared for you?"

"Almost," he responded, "but I want to start now. I don't want to waste any more time."

Mrs. Ochoa turned and walked to a small table in the corner of the class that looked like it was about to crumble under its own fragility. On top of the table were five rusty cans of paint, five brushes, all of which ranged in size, and a small plastic tray.

"Only five colors?"

"I see you haven't yet reached the chart showing you how to mix a few colors to make many new colors," Mrs. Ochoa replied.

He approached the rickety table. Each can of paint was so rusted it looked like it had been doused with dirty honey. The only way he was able to distinguish the colors inside each can was through a small, crude streak of blue, yellow, red, black and white, running just above each can's dilapidated label.

"How can I make many colors with just these ones?"

Mrs. Ochoa pointed at the plastic tray. It was a black, shallow, dusty basin. Francisco grabbed it and blew into it, a small cloud of dreary grey dust floated away. He shook the tray to get the rest of the dust out, but the flexibility of the flimsy plastic was too drastic. Scared it would break, he put it back on the table.

"What can I do with this thing?"

"You use it to mix the paint together, to make whatever color you wish," Mrs. Ochoa said.

"With this?" he said. "If I pour a whole can of paint into this, it'll break."

Mrs. Ochoa smiled reassuringly.

"You don't need to empty a whole can into it," she said. "Once you get started, you'll realize you don't even need that much paint at all. That tray will serve you well, you'll see."

"What am I supposed mix the paint with, my finger?" He followed his words with a spirited chuckle.

Mrs. Ochoa, taking no offense at his sarcasm, responded, "You use this." She picked up a long, flat wooden stick resting quietly on the table. It looked like an oversized tongue depressor. Francisco laughed. But, when Mrs. Ochoa simulated the mixing action within the empty plastic tray, he nodded approvingly. Facing the five cans of paint, Francisco randomly chose the color red. He picked the can up. It was heavy and sealed. He looked back at Mrs. Ochoa, who handed him what looked like a curved, steel thumb. "This is to open the cans," she said.

He placed the can down and accepted the metallic thumb. It was hard with coarse skin. He held the thumb with one hand and wrapped the fingers of his other hand around the can of red paint. He wedged the thumb under the can's lid and popped it open. He put the thumb in his pocket, where it joined Ms. Espinosa's inflated bill. He removed the lid, flipped it over, placed it down on the table and looked at the open can. The red paint rested peacefully.

"It's oil based," Mrs. Ochoa said, "so it's tough, and won't wash away, chip or fade in the rain."

Francisco lowered his face to the red paint, inadvertently inhaling its fumes. His eyes blurred then moistened. He felt lightheaded. He placed the lid back on, pushed it down and took a step back. After regaining his equilibrium, he gazed at the can of paint timorously, showing it the respect it deserved.

He looked at the five brushes. He picked up the largest one. The bristles were stiff and stubborn. He wrapped his fingers around the inflexible strands of yellow, desiccated straw and squeezed them in an attempt to assert control, but the brush's shriveled mane felt so dry he believed any kind of friction, from the stingiest rub to the faintest breath, would set it ablaze. He looked up at Mrs. Ochoa, who stood close by, watching attentively.

"Once you dip it in the paint, the bristles will loosen," she said.

"But they're so dry."

"They haven't been used in a long, long time, Francisco, but don't worry, the paint will rehydrate them."

Still holding the brush in his hand, Francisco rotated his wrist, assessing the balance of the tool, gauging its weight and feel. The handle was smooth, but chipped at the bottom.

"That will be your main brush," the teacher said. "It's perfect for long, broad, body strokes."

He placed the largest brush atop the table. He picked up the smallest of the five brushes. It was nearly weightless. Its handle was smooth, much like the large brush, but lacked its scars. He grazed the small brush's tiny head against the back of his hand. The bristles were soft, tickling his skin.

"That brush is for precision, for the smaller, more specific details you need in order to give your portraits life, like the hair, pupils, veins and blemishes."

Francisco placed the small brush back on the table. He looked at the other three brushes and ran the back of his hand along their beards. Their bristles were a compromise between the rigid brutishness of the largest brush and the soft conspicuousness of the smallest one.

"Those are your tools," Mrs. Ochoa said. "Everything you need."

Francisco flung his knapsack over his shoulder, pulled out the notebook she wrote for him, held it in front of her and said, "*Now* I have everything I need."

She smiled.

Francisco knelt down, put the knapsack on the floor, put the notebook back inside and without looking up he said, "How am I supposed to get all of this stuff outside?"

A door slammed shut. Mrs. Ochoa was gone. Francisco stood, took a step and nearly tripped. He looked down. The shoelace on one of his shiny black shoes was undone. He bent down and tied the disobedient black string. A squealing sound was heard from outside the classroom. He stood straight, but there was still no sign of his favorite teacher.

"Mrs. Ochoa?"

The squealing persisted. Like a haunting moan, the sound, muffled by the walls, was steady in its anguish. It grew progressively louder. It was getting closer.

"Mrs. Ochoa?"

There was no answer, just the steady sound of the twisted squealing.

He looked down at his watch and pushed every single one of the little buttons surrounding its face. He looked at the gashes in his knees behind the torn fabric of his pants. He looked at his shoes and studied the bow he had just tied. He looked at his knapsack resting on the floor. He looked at the splintered leg of a nearby desk. He heard the classroom door open. The source of the squealing was now inside, moaning louder than before. His eyes kept searching for things to occupy his vision and distract his mind from having to see whatever created the horrifying sound.

"Francisco."

Silencing the tormented squealing, Mrs. Ochoa's voice made his name sound sweeter than ever before. He looked up. She was standing at the doorway and in front of her was a table. It was similar to the decrepit table housing his supplies, except it had two levels and four small wheels for feet.

"This is the only table with wheels in the school. I took it from the empty classroom across the hall. You can use it to take everything to the wall outside."

She pushed the table to the center of the room. The squealing recommenced, as all four of the table's wheels turned. All of the terror Francisco associated with the dreadful sound disappeared however, as he found a way to unveil the face of fear only to discover a cheerful smile, a set of compassionate eyes and a benign voice.

With Mrs. Ochoa's help, Francisco placed his arsenal on both levels of the table. He put the cans of paint on the bottom level, each one eliciting a strained creak from the table's frame. The brushes were spread out atop one-half of the upper level of the table, each one given sufficient space to breath, while the plastic tray rested on the other half, with the wooden stir stick inside.

"Are you ready?" Mrs. Ochoa asked.

Francisco picked up his knapsack, slung it securely over his shoulder and said, "I hope so."

He approached the mobile table, placed both his hands on each corner, spun himself and the table around and pushed it toward the doorway. The table's wheels obeyed and rotated, each one squealing loudly. Mrs. Ochoa walked in front of him and opened the door. He thanked his favorite teacher and pushed the table out of the classroom. Just as he exited the room, he felt a soft squeeze from a comforting hand gripping his shoulder. He turned. Mrs. Ochoa was facing him, and in her other hand was a large jug of water.

"I almost forgot this," she said. "You'll need it to wash off the brushes after you use them, for the times you don't want the colors to mix."

"Thank you," he said.

"When you're finished, just bring the table back. I'll store all your tools safely in my class and you can come back whenever you need them. My door will always be open to you, Francisco."

He thanked her again, accepted the large jug of water and rested it on the bottom half of the table. He walked in the center of the hallway, the wheels' squealing blasting through the cavernous corridor, reverberating throughout. Suddenly, the same fat security guard who stopped him earlier in the day stood in front of him, forcing him to stop. The guard took a break from eating an overstuffed sandwich and said, "Where are you going? Why are you pushing that table? And why are you making such a racket? Teachers are complaining about it, saying it's disturbing their lessons."

"I'm going to my gym class."

Francisco pushed the table, but the guard stopped him after two steps, slapping his chubby hands on it, disturbing the carefully coordinated positions of the paintbrushes. Francisco looked at the door he wished to pass through then looked at the guard hindering his progress.

"What's the problem?" he asked. "That's my next class."

The guard looked at him suspiciously.

"Maybe, but why are you taking all of this stuff with you?"

"Ms. Espinosa told me I have to paint the school's surrounding wall, and I decided to start here. We can take it up with her if you don't believe me."

The guard gazed at him, took a bite of his sandwich and said, "Fine, go ahead, but do something about that table's noise." The guard shuffled back, opened the door, moved aside and allowed Francisco to pass.

Outside the sun was bright, and the air was still. Francisco looked around. Students stood in the center of the paved field in front of the stocky supply teacher. None of them noticed Francisco and his table until he started walking toward the wall, and the table's wheels started squealing again.

"Where are you going?" the supply teacher said.

"I'm going to the wall over there that I have to paint," Francisco casually replied, as if his intentions were perfectly normal. Not bothering to wait for a response, he walked away, pushing the table in front of him.

Once he reached the wall that encased the school, Francisco stopped, rested the table by his side, slung his knapsack over his shoulder and dropped it to the ground. He looked up, the blankness of the wall was stunning. He picked up the largest of the five brushes, the body brush. He bent over and looked at the five cans of paint, each one's color declaring itself through the small streak above the can's faded label. Black? No. Yellow? Why? Blue? Of course not. Red? Ridiculous. White? No. None of the colors fit what he needed. He knelt down, grabbed his knapsack, reached his hand inside and pulled out the notebook with Mrs. Ochoa's notes. He opened it and flipped through the pages. He found what he was looking for on the final page: a flowing hierarchy with the five colors of the cans he possessed resting at the top. Spanning the entire page, in small, but legible writing, along with tiny color filled squares, the chart detailed which colors should be mixed to make, as Francisco saw, and Mrs. Ochoa had told him earlier, many different colors.

The first set of mixtures presented Francisco with several colors he needed, brown in particular, which came from mixing red paint and green paint, which came from mixing blue paint and yellow paint. Further down the page, he was surprised to see that some mixtures did not involve any of the original five colors, but were created from mixtures mixed with other mixtures, rendering the original five colors powerless and obsolete. By the time he reached the bottommost colors of the chart, Francisco counted well over thirty-five colors in total. Looking over the chart again, it was difficult for him to believe the more established, elder colors at the top had any bond, any link, any control over the more innovative, vibrant, youthful colors at the bottom.

He looked back up at the blank, concrete wall that was to be his canvas. He pulled the curved, metal thumb out of his pocket and propped it under the lids of the cans required to create the colors he needed. After mixing the necessary colors in the tray, he dipped the body brush into a freshly created brown pool and raised it. Long drops of syrupy paint streamed down, returning to the source from whence they came. He turned and took two steps toward the wall, leaving a thin trail of paint on the pavement below. He thrust the brush forward, powerfully, but was just short of making contact with the wall, when his face suddenly went as blank as the wall itself.

Who am I supposed to paint first?

The first name that came to mind was Veronika, but from that answer came the more difficult question as to whom he was going to paint second, third, fourth, fifth, ninety-second. He turned around, took two steps back to the table, placed the body brush back into the thick pool of brown paint and looked at the crowd of students huddled in front of the supply teacher. He couldn't hear what they were saying. All he could see was the majority of them, girls and boys alike, mindlessly giggling amongst themselves. He heard a loud gasp from behind. He turned. Crouched down, breathing heavy, was a student he recognized, but whose name he could not recall. The student shared the same grade as him however, and that's all he needed. Taller, bigger, more athletic than Francisco, the student's current fragile condition betrayed his powerful physique. He approached his winded peer. Not noticing him, the student continued petitioning for air.

"Are you okay?" Francisco asked.

The student sprang up defensively.

"I'm fine."

Not knowing how to begin the conversation, Francisco said, "Can I ask you for a favor?"

The student glared at him suspiciously and replied, "It depends what you want."

"I just need to ask you some questions," Francisco said. "It's for something I have to do for Ms. Espinosa."

The student sneered. His nostrils flared. His chest bulged. His forearms rippled.

"You're helping Ms. Espinosa?" the student said.

"Helping her? *Hell no,*" Francisco replied.

"Good, because anybody who helps her is just as bad as she is."

"She's making me do a stupid project," Francisco said, "and she says if I don't do it, I'm going to be expelled, and my next year's tuition will be forfeited. I know she can't actually do it, but—"

"Of course she'll do it," the student interrupted. "She'll expel you. She'll keep your tuition. And she'll laugh in your face when she's done."

The student spoke with a tone of clarity rooted in what Francisco feared to be certainty.

"So what do you have to ask me?" the student said.

Francisco had no idea what he had to ask. He had no idea what questions he needed to learn enough about a person to paint them, so he asked the first one that came to mind.

"What do you love about this school?"

The student looked at Francisco oddly, took a moment and replied blandly, providing the kind of answer that could have been given by any student at any time. After hearing the student's dull response, all Francisco could see himself painting was a lifeless stick figure. Impatience announced its presence on the student's face. Francisco thought of a second, and hopefully better question.

"Okay," he said. "What do you *hate* about this school?"

The student's face lit up, "Evil."

Francisco looked at the student quizzically, "Evil?"

"Yes," the student replied, "Evil Espinosa."

"Cool name," Francisco said, "Did you make it up?"

It was the student's turn to offer Francisco a perplexed expression before replying, "Everybody calls her that. Didn't you know that?"

"No."

The student's eyes grew deeper, more effervescent, his hair more distinguishable, down to the last strand. Everything about the student suddenly appeared unique and detailed, right down to the scattered pimples on his face. Not wanting to lose the momentum that without him even knowing it possessed his hand to move around as if he was painting the student without a brush in its grasp, Francisco was about to follow up his second, far more effective question, when the student asked a question of his own.

"You want to know what I hate most about Evil?" he said.

"Of course," Francisco replied.

The student explained, in furious detail, how the school's soccer team, which he was the captain of, qualified for a national tournament, but was unable to participate because Ms. Espinosa denied the funding necessary to charter a bus.

"She said the money was best suited to go somewhere else," the student said. "Didn't you hear about that?"

"No," Francisco replied as he was barely aware of any of the school's teams' existences, let alone their financial situations.

The student continued, telling Francisco the team would have won the tournament, easily, and the victory would have helped every member gain the kind of national recognition every student athlete dreams of, while also shining a bright light on the school itself.

"She said the school didn't need any bright lights shining on it."

Continuing with his story, the student explained why he was running to the point of exhaustion.

"After Evil shut down the tournament, almost half the team quit, so I was told I had to train even harder."

Francisco asked the student why so many members of his team left.

"They said there wasn't any point in playing so well if nobody was going to see it."

As the student kept talking, Francisco sketched his profile in his mind, catching every contour, while glancing every few seconds at the space on the surrounding wall where he intended to paint him. With the student showing no signs of slowing down, Francisco ached to start painting, his glances at the wall growing ever more frequent. He wished every word the student uttered would signal the conclusion of his story.

Two seconds of silence elapsed. Unsure if that was the signal he had hoped for, Francisco, not wanting to take any chances, said, "Wow, I knew Ms. Espinosa—"

"*Evil*," the student interrupted.

"Sorry, I knew Evil was bad, but I didn't know she was *that* bad."

He was about to add to his comment, when the student said, "Talk to anybody in this school, and I'm sure they'll have their own story about what she's done to them. I bet a lot of them are probably worse than mine."

Francisco's doubts now vastly outweighed the weakening belief that Ms. Espinosa couldn't do what she said she would do if he didn't finish the portraits on time.

"I have to get back to training," the student said. "We only have half-a-team now, and I don't want to get destroyed in our next game."

The student took three long strides away, stopped, turned and said, "Hey, I forgot to ask, what is it you have to do for this project?"

Francisco wanted to lie, but couldn't convince himself to be dishonest to somebody who was so honest with him.

"I have to paint you, and everybody else in our grade."

The student looked at Francisco oddly, just as Francisco feared he would, but then smiled and said, "And you have to do it for Evil, right? You're doing it for her to see?"

Francisco nodded.

"Then can you do me a favor?"

Francisco said he would, anticipating some sort of superficial request, from making his muscles look bigger, to making sure his hair looked good, to painting his face with no pimples, but the student's request was much simpler, and much stranger.

"Make sure I'm smiling, no, *laughing*, and when you paint my eyes, paint them red, *flaming* red."

Francisco asked why, and the student replied, "Because I hate Evil and I want her, and everybody else who sees the painting, to see that hate in my eyes."

"Why the laughing?"

"I want her to see me laughing in her face because I can't think of anything that would piss her off more."

Francisco said he would fulfill the request. The student thanked him, and ran off.

With the largest of the five brushes still resting within the pool of brown paint, Francisco grabbed the brush's chipped handle, pulled it out, approached the wall and struck it with a potent thrust.

After an hour passed, Francisco stepped back, in front of him was a headless figure, an incomplete duplicate of the student he had spoken to earlier. The height, width and girth were spot on. The accuracy of the student's skin tone was heightened by the various small blotches of discoloration every human's flesh possessed. Even though he wasn't wearing it at the time, Francisco painted the student in uniform, making sure the strict spotlessness of his jet black shoes and the luminous glisten of the school's golden crest on his blue shirt were impeccably intact.

The portrait's multi-dimensional likeness swelled from the wall. Never before had a headless person stood so confidently. With his fingers clasped around his hips, the student's portrait stood waiting. Francisco looked back at the table, every can of paint was popped open, four of the five brushes were soaked with water. In the tray were several small pools of differently colored mixtures.

Francisco's wrist ached, his head throbbed, and his eyes strained. He took a deep breath. When he inhaled, the dizzying scent of paint was all he could smell. Sweat bubbled just beneath his hairline. He wiped his forehead with the back of his hand. The combination of sweat and drying paint felt like slime. He spit. He stared at the headless portrait, not admiring it, but studying it.

He picked up the smallest of the five paintbrushes, its bristles stiff and spotless. He dipped the brush into one of the tray's colorful lagoons, and raised the small brush close enough to his eye to see each bristle's lathered tip. He approached the portrait that anxiously anticipated the addition of one of the body's most crucial components. Unlike the forceful thrust he used earlier with the largest of the five brushes, with the smallest brush he lightly grazed the wall with a tempered touch.

Another hour passed. The paint on the back of Francisco's hand, along with the paint smeared across his forehead, was starting to crust. He smiled, and the student's portrait smiled back at him, the student's replicated face an expression of precision, right down to the pores. Even the portrait's hair appeared to move in the blowing wind.

In spite of the stunning similarities between the portrait and its subject, one crucial element was absent. Even though the portrait laughed, it could not yet see. Francisco approached the opened can of red paint. He washed the smallest of the five brushes' mane with the last drops of water from the large jug and dipped its cleansed tip directly into the can. No mixture was required for what he was going to paint next. He would use the full, pure passion of the livid color. When he pulled the brush out, the entirety of its bristles were bright red.

His stomach was grumbling. With the lunch hour concluding moments ago, and Francisco ignoring it in favor of finishing his first portrait, the inevitable pangs of hunger roared within his gut. Silencing his stomach's incessant demands for nourishment, he raised the small brush and aimed it at the portrait's empty eye sockets. With the tip of the brush millimeters away from the wall, the ache plaguing his wrist for the last two hours grew worse. His hand shook. His vision started betraying him. A combination of intense concentration and paint fumes caused everything around him to blur. He bent down and took several deep breaths, while carefully cradling the brush between his fingers, when a frightening question suddenly entered his mind.

How am I ever going to finish ninety-one more of these in less than two-and-a-half weeks?

Without answering, he stood straight, raised his hand once again and willed it forward. The tips of the brush's strands gently touched the portrait's face.

Twenty minutes passed. Francisco took a step back. The portrait's eyes, big and bold, deep and wide open, flaming with crimson rage, trapped him, tied him up, demanded his attention and told him their story.

7.

The next morning, dressed in his alternate pair of pants, Francisco walked into Ms. Espinosa's office. He had already gotten his textbook from Ms. Vasquez, and he reminded himself several times during the journey from her class to the office to not forget to return it before the beginning of the day's second period. He took the book out of his knapsack and placed it on his desk with a loud slap. He dropped his knapsack, reached into his pocket, pulled out a wad of cash, approached Ms. Espinosa's desk and dropped the money. The principal, who was shifting through some papers, looked up just enough to see the cash, but not enough to see Francisco's face. Her hand shot forward, snatching the money. She counted it, fluttering each bill with her fingers, rubbing the currency with her nails. He stared at the cash his parents gave him, imagining a million different things that could have been done with the money, all considerably more appealing than finding it within the clutches of Ms. Espinosa's sordid hands.

"So when do I get my new pants?" he asked.

Ms. Espinosa put all the money in one hand, and with her eyes still focused on the cash, she waved her other hand at the door, as if she had the ability to summarily dismiss the very air Francisco breathed.

"Ask the secretary, she'll tell you how to order them."

He turned, but stopped after Ms. Espinosa told him to wait. He paused, and watched as she scribbled something on a small piece of paper before ordering him to take it. He cautiously stepped forward, grabbed the paper and gazed at the amount written at the bottom of it.

"But I just paid you."

The principal looked at Francisco, and smiled.

"Right now you're paying for the desk you broke, the fine for the book you returned late, and the penalty for walking around the school with a torn uniform. As for the actual purchasing of new pants, that is a completely separate charge."

Like a fighter taking a heavy punch to the ribs, Francisco stumbled, anxious to throw a haymaking response.

"You have no idea how hard it was for me to convince my parents to not show up here this morning," he said. "They were furious at the amount you charged them. If I show them another bill, I don't think I can prevent them from coming into your office, and when they do, they won't hold back."

Ms. Espinosa leaned back in her throne, absorbing the power of his strike with ease.

"That would be unfortunate," she replied.

"Yeah it would," he said.

"It would be unfortunate because if your parents did decide to come here and *not hold back*, as you so bluntly put it, I'd have no choice but to do the same."

Suspicious, Francisco responded with a jabbing question as to what exactly she meant, to which she countered, "As the school's principal, one of my primary jobs is to keep parents informed about their children, and in your case, I'm sure your parents would be interested to know about the specifics of a certain project you have only two-and-a-half weeks left to complete."

Francisco parried the blow by shrugging his shoulders and replying, "They already know about it, and they told me to do my best. They even told me I could stay an hour after school every day starting tomorrow to do it."

As if his reply wasn't even uttered, let alone heard, the principal said, "I think they would particularly like to know what happens if their son doesn't complete the project, something I would have no choice but to tell them, in detail, since nobody would be holding back."

Francisco's eyes bulged as if struck by a punch he never saw coming.

Ms. Espinosa threw her hands up and slapped them flat on her desk, before adding, "Of course, I'm sure they already know exactly what would happen if you don't complete those portraits, right? I would just be repeating what I'm sure you've already told them, right? I would be wasting my time, right?"

Francisco remained silent.

"Oh," Ms. Espinosa said. "So you *didn't* tell your parents what would happen if you don't finish those portraits?"

Francisco licked his suddenly dried lips and replied, "You can't do that. You can't just keep their money."

"Did you think I was bluffing, Francisco?" she said. "Of course I can do it, and I will, just as easily as I come and go in and out of this school."

"Then you'd just be stealing," he said.

"I don't see it that way."

"What other way do you see it?"

"Certainly not that one," she said.

"Please, Ms. Espinosa."

She leaned back in her throne.

"I love hearing you say that word, Francisco, I really do. I must be lucky, what is this, the second? No, the *third* time you've said please to me this week."

She gave Francisco another heaping portion of her ruthless grin, adding to the degradation of the knock-out blow he'd just suffered. Dazed, Francisco stuffed the bill into his pocket. He realized the principal knew all along he wouldn't tell his parents about the consequences of his inability to finish the portraits, that the threat of their intervention was nothing more than a gun without bullets, a dull blade, a useless hope. His head sank. He would get no help. He was alone. And as he stared at the spotless floor beneath his feet, he realized he had no choice but to finish the portraits.

"Good," Ms. Espinosa said. "Now, is there anything else you have to tell me?"

He looked up.

"Yes," he said. "I finished the first portrait yesterday, and it's perfect."

Fondling the cash Francisco gave her, Ms. Espinosa said, "That's great, but you still have ninety-one left to go, and seeing how you no longer have any doubts as to what will happen if you don't finish, I suggest you work faster."

Francisco didn't respond.

"Now go take care of those pants," she said, her eyes still focused on his parent's money.

Without saying a word, Francisco turned his back and made his way to the secretary's desk. He asked her about getting new pants. The secretary, typing as madly as ever, paused, looked up, scowled and said, "Fill this out." She slid a tiny piece of paper asking for Francisco's waistline size, which he didn't know, the length he wanted for the pants, which he didn't know, and whether or not he wanted the pants hemmed, which he didn't know.

"Do I have to fill this out now?"

"Yes."

He responded to each question randomly, caring little about what the pants would look like when they arrived, if they would arrive at all. He slid the form back toward the secretary, who snatched it from him with rough, calloused fingertips that scraped the top of his hand, chafing it, scourging the skin. He'd been saving whatever money he could scrounge up over the course of the school year, from his allowance from his parents, gifts on his birthday and other holidays from his family, even money he'd found on the ground, all in hopes he could use it over the summer. He pulled the makeshift bill out of his pocket, did the math, and realized he had just enough to pay it, leaving him with nothing. He stuffed the bill back into his pocket, turned and walked back into Ms. Espinosa's office. He glanced at the principal's desk. The money he gave her was nowhere to be seen. Francisco, sitting at his desk, opened the textbook Ms. Vasquez gave him and stared at the pages' words blankly. All he could think about were the portraits he had to paint. After five minutes of trying to figure out a way he could finish all of the portraits before the pending deadline, he looked up at Ms. Espinosa, who was reading from a collection of papers laid out in front of her.

"Ms. Espinosa." He paused, making a last attempt to figure out an alternative to what he was going to ask, but found none. "Can I *please* work on the portraits during the day as well as during gym class and after school?"

The principal looked back at him, smiled and replied, "I'm glad to see you're taking imitative, Francisco. Of course you can work on the portraits during the day."

"And my classes?"

The principal, whose focus returned to the papers in front of her, said, "Don't worry about your classes."

"Can I start now?" he asked.

"Go."

He got up from his seat, painfully said thank you, slammed the textbook shut, stuffed it in his knapsack and dashed out of Ms. Espinosa's office.

After dropping off his book in Ms. Vasquez's classroom without saying a word to the teacher, or receiving a word from her, Francisco made his way to Mrs. Ochoa's classroom.

Mrs. Ochoa, who was standing at the front of the class, pointing at the chalkboard describing a drawing method Francisco remembered from the notes she wrote for him, turned to him and smiled. He did his best to reciprocate the pleasant gesture, but the worry in his mind flooded his lips making them too heavy to crest upwards into a smile. He pointed at his table of supplies resting at the rear of the class. The teacher nodded, told her students to hold on for a moment and asked Francisco to step outside.

Once outside the classroom, Mrs. Ochoa stood close to him. "What's wrong?" she said in a cautioned whisper. Speaking in an equally hushed voice, he replied, "You were right. Everybody was right. I can't believe I thought she couldn't do it. She'll expel me, *and* she'll keep my parents' money."

"Not if you finish the portraits."

He looked up at Mrs. Ochoa.

"But that's the problem."

"What do you mean?"

"I don't know who to paint next."

"How many portraits have you painted already?" she asked.

"Just one, somebody from my gym class," he responded, "and I only have two-and-a-half weeks to finish ninety-one more."

"What inspired you to paint the student from your gym class?"

"We just started talking."

"What did you talk about?"

He told the teacher how ineffective it was when he asked the student what he loved about the school, but how helpful it was after he asked the student what he hated about it. Mrs. Ochoa questioned him about the student's response. He told her the student's story revolved around Evil.

Mrs. Ochoa looked both ways, making sure nobody was around, "Espinosa?"

"You know about that name, too?" he asked, doing all he could to maintain the secretive tone of voice they both shared.

"Of course," she said. "Everybody knows about that name."

"I didn't."

The kindly teacher leaned closer to him, making sure none of her words fell into the wrong ears, "It's not just students who call her that." She pulled her head back and smiled at him.

"When the guy I was talking to told me why he hated Evil, and how much he hated her, I was able to sketch him in my mind, and when he left, I took everything in my head, and using a lot of the things I read in the notebook you gave me, I painted him on the wall. It took me around two hours."

"I think you already found the solution to your problem, Francisco."

Mrs. Ochoa took a step back, opened her classroom door and walked in. Francisco eagerly followed close behind. Once inside, he gazed at the seated students, all of whom were in the same grade as him. Some of the students were immersed in conversations with their friends; others read the books opened in front of them, while the majority of them just stared at the walls.

He turned to Mrs. Ochoa, who took a step forward and addressed the students, "Francisco has a problem, and I think everybody here can help him."

The conversations amongst the seated students stopped, books closed, blank stares were replaced with inquisitive glares. Firmly holding the attention of her students, Mrs. Ochoa continued, "Francisco is going to conduct interviews with each of you, one at a time. They shouldn't take more than a few minutes."

Mrs. Ochoa stepped aside, leaving Francisco alone at the front of the class. He looked at his peers. There was nothing about them he could cling to, capture and transport to the large grey wall surrounding the school.

"Who would like to go first?" Mrs. Ochoa asked.

Timid whispers floated throughout the room.

"I'll go first," a student seated in the front row said. The student stood. Tall but skinny, energetic but nervous, the boy spoke in a shrill voice. Francisco recognized the student from a recent encounter, but couldn't remember where and when it took place. "Where do we go?" the student asked.

"The empty classroom across the hall from this one" Mrs. Ochoa said. "Room 115."

"Isn't that classroom locked?" the student said. "We can't go into locked classrooms."

"Don't worry about that," she replied.

Francisco watched the student approach the door with weak strides. Francisco followed him, but stopped in front of Mrs. Ochoa, who reasserted herself at the front of the class. He turned to her and whispered, "Are you sure this is okay? Won't you get into trouble for letting students use an empty, locked classroom?" The teacher looked at Francisco, smiled, reached into her pocket, pulled out a key and handed it to him.

Outside of Mrs. Ochoa's class, awaiting Francisco, standing in front of the door leading to the empty classroom neither of them had entered before, was the tall, gangly student. His body was shaking.

"What's wrong?" Francisco asked.

The student looked down both ends of the hallway, before replying, "Are you sure we can go into this classroom? Are you sure we won't get in trouble? I don't want to go to Evil's office."

Francisco assured the student nothing would happen, that they, and every other student in the class, heard Mrs. Ochoa say he was allowed to conduct interviews within the empty classroom. The student's quaking ceased, but his anxiety remained, painted all over his face. Francisco opened his hand, exposing the small key Mrs. Ochoa gave him. It was the same length as the iron thumb he used to open his cans of paint. He pushed the key into the narrow slit in the center of the rusted doorknob, took a deep breath and turned it. The knob rotated. There was a click and the door yielded. He pushed it open and took a step forward. With the safety and comfort of light glowing behind him and the ambiguity and appetite of darkness awaiting him ahead, he walked into the room. Will, the fuel that powers pursuit, enabled him to take another step into the void, when, with the utterance of the word *oops*, followed by the sound of a door slamming shut, the light behind him was extinguished and he was enveloped by the darkness.

Inside the dark chamber, Francisco was accosted by a rank, musty odor. Unable to see anything in front, beside or behind him, he proceeded further until he bumped into something. He cautiously extended his hand and grazed the tip of his index finger along the surface of what he believed to be a desk. The room illuminated. He turned and saw the scrawny student standing by a small plastic panel. He raised his finger, the tip covered with a thick layer of grey dust.

The similarity between this classroom and the other classrooms within the school was uncanny. There were four parallel rows of desks with chairs tightly pushed behind them. There was a large desk at the front of the class with a blank chalkboard, an empty garbage can, a ticking clock and a portrait of Ms. Espinosa resting comfortably on a wooden mantel, above everything, staring down. Despite having everything it needed to function however, the classroom remained unused, draped in a sheet of seclusion and neglect.

Francisco was about to occupy the large, vacant desk that was reserved for teachers, but changed his mind when he saw his peer instinctively sit in one of the small, uncomfortable, dusty desks reserved for students. Francisco joined his peer and sat in the desk next to him. He looked around. The room was unusually bright. Equipped with the same dim, weakened lighting as every other classroom within the school, Francisco didn't understand what made this classroom any different until he realized the confined light above was amplified by the wraiths of dust covering every desk below.

Staring at Francisco, the student appeared eager for the inquiry to come. He hoped the student, whose name he still didn't know, wouldn't be disappointed at being asked a single, simple question.

"Before I start the interview," he said. "What's your name?"

"Gabriel," the student said.

"I actually have only one question for you Gabriel," Francisco said, "but I think it will help me with what I have to do."

"What *do* you have to do?"

Francisco paused, and after carefully considering what kind of response he would receive as a result of his answer, he replied, "I have to paint you, and everybody else in our grade."

Gabriel reacted much differently than Francisco anticipated by not reacting at all. He just remained in his seat, ready for the question, as if being painted by a student he barely knew was the most normal thing in the world.

"What do you hate about this school?" Francisco asked.

Gabriel looked up, then around the brightly lit classroom. His body betrayed none of his thoughts. Francisco had no idea what kind of reply he was going to receive.

"I hate the food served in the cafeteria."

Unimpressed, Francisco hoped to receive the same kind of elaborate answer given by the student he ran into during gym class, but luck can be a tempestuous thing. He looked at Gabriel, scrutinizing him, trying to find something, anything to cling to, but couldn't sketch him, couldn't bring him to life. He started to stand, the creaking of his desk exposing his movements, when Gabriel added, "It's rotten. I ate some chicken in there a few days ago, and I knew it was still raw because I could see some blood in the middle of it, but I was so hungry. Anyway, it made me sick, but there was nothing I could do about it until I got home."

Francisco finally remembered where he recognized Gabriel from: he was the student devouring the bloodied chicken next to him, while he waited for Veronika inside the cafeteria a few days earlier.

"Why couldn't you do anything until you got home?" Francisco questioned after sitting back down.

Gabriel looked at him peculiarly, as if an answer was not necessary, as if he should have known why.

"Because there's no nurse in the school."

Francisco responded with a surprised huff. He had never been sick within the school's walls, so he never needed to know if there was a nurse or not. He'd also never eaten the cafeteria's food either.

"When I went to the office and told Evil the chicken from the cafeteria made me sick, she told me it was my fault. She told me I was sick from the food I ate at home, the food my mom made for my breakfast. When I told her I didn't eat breakfast, that my mom was already at work when I woke up, she said I got sick because I didn't eat in the morning."

Francisco noticed the furrows in Gabriel's forehead grow deeper. Gabriel continued his story, telling Francisco how Ms. Espinosa told him he wasn't sick at all, that he was making it up, that he just wanted to get out of class. Finally, when he was no longer able to contain the sickness Ms. Espinosa told him did not exist, he vomited on her flawlessly polished floor.

"She told me to clean it up," he said. "She told me to get down on my hands and knees, like a dog."

"Did you?" Francisco asked.

Gabriel remained quiet. Shame swept through the room. He nodded his head, "I said no at first, but she told me I had no choice, that if I didn't do it, I'd be suspended," Gabriel replied. "I told her it smelled horrible. She told me to put my face closer to it so I could smell it even more, so I would know to never do it again."

In an act of inquisitive reflex, Francisco looked down at the floor of the classroom, imagining having to do what Gabriel was ordered to do.

"I told her I didn't have anything to clean it with, so she asked me if I had an undershirt. I said yes, but I wish I said no. She told me to use it to clean up my mess because she didn't want me to stain my uniform and disrespect the school crest."

As Gabriel's head sank, Francisco noticed the glistening pores of his cheeks and the slightly elfish points at the tips of his ears, but most of all, he noticed the emptiness of his eyes. Gabriel took a long, deep breath, then raised his head and said loudly, angrily, "After I stood up, I took off my uniform shirt then the undershirt, and Evil just stood there, laughing at me, telling me I was the boniest kid she'd ever seen in her life."

With the echo of his words bouncing off the classroom's walls, Gabriel added, "After that, I got back down on my hands and knees and started cleaning, wiping up my own puke with my undershirt, while Evil just stood there, telling me to scrub harder. That's all she said, over and over, *Scrub harder. Scrub harder. Scrub harder.*"

Francisco looked around, expecting somebody to walk in and investigate the source of the booming voice roaring throughout the room, but nobody came. Gabriel continued explaining the putrid cleaning process he was forced to undertake, while gesticulating his points ferociously. His face reddened. His nostrils flared. His eyes filled with rage. He abruptly stood. Appearing much taller, his chest, though small and lacking any distinguishable girth, heaved forward with every word. The shrillness of his voice vanished. His tone was gruffer, harsher with every degrading addition to his story. Bringing Gabriel to life was no longer a challenge for Francisco, but an effortless endeavor, and with an innate ease, he sketched him in his mind.

"After I finally cleaned it up, Evil told me to keep the shirt I used because she didn't want me putting it in her garbage can where she'd have to smell it. Then she told me to get to class, and not to say anything to anybody about the chicken they served in the cafeteria, and if she found out that I did, I'd be suspended."

Gabriel's concluding words were not spoken, but growled, making him sound like the animal Ms. Espinosa reduced him to during the ordeal he so intensely described. After he was finished, Gabriel stood, "I hope I was able to help you," he said. He then walked toward the door, grabbed the knob, turned it and quietly shuffled his way out of the room, while his sketched duplicate ran wild within the walls of Francisco's mind, wailing for release.

In a stupor, Francisco sat by himself inside the empty classroom. He slouched in the small chair behind the dusty desk. With his eyes glazed over by the gleaming light reflecting off the sheets of dust, he closed his eyes and breathed in. The dank classroom's odor was fetid. With his eyes still shut, he leaned back in his chair. A loud creak was the only sound heard as the chair's two front feet levitated. After several moments, Francisco's serenity was interrupted when he heard the opening of the classroom door. His eyes opened. The chair's front feet slammed on the filthy floor. He glared at the doorway, where yet another student stood.

When the bell rang, the period was over. Following Gabriel's interview, Francisco had been able to complete six more. He stood from the chair he occupied throughout the hour-long period, and rested both of his hands on the dusty desk, creating a set of grungy palm and finger prints. He turned off the light as he exited the classroom. Outside the room he was surrounded by a surge of students rushing past him, galloping down the school's main hallway. None of the students looked around. All of their faces were directed straight ahead, aimed at their next class. Next Francisco walked back into Mrs. Ochoa's classroom. There were only five students seated at their desks, with more trickling in. The teacher looked at Francisco and asked him if he was tired.

"No," he replied.

"Are you sure?" She said. "You look exhausted."

Student after student, interview after interview, left Francisco's mind in a state of inspired fatigue. The collection of sketched images he ached to paint bombarded his brain, bullying it, bashing his senses. They fervently pushed and shoved their way to the forefront, as if they were all trapped in a building engulfed in flames.

"I just have a lot on my mind."

He stepped closer to his favorite teacher and spoke in the same tone of voice reminiscent of the clandestine conversation they had earlier.

"I can't believe the things I heard, and I only did seven interviews, eight if you include the guy I talked to in gym class," he said. "I didn't know this kind of stuff was happening."

He told Mrs. Ochoa how one student, an overweight girl named Carmen, told him she hated having her period because the first one she had was in class, and she stained a chair with her blood. She told Francisco how the principal, whom he now referred to as Evil, as he could no longer call her by any other name, ridiculed her by saying she was bleeding out like a stuck pig then proceeded to make her parents buy a new chair, saying she refused to have her school polluted by Carmen's filthy emission.

"I couldn't believe they were telling me these things," he said, "but after I told them I had to paint them on the school's surrounding wall, they just let it all out, and I have been able to sketch them all, each and every one of them, in my mind."

Mrs. Ochoa stared at him, but didn't respond.

He continued by revealing the miserable tale of Manuel, a short, mousy boy with a pair of small, slim eyes, who told Francisco he hated the bruises covering his body. Francisco described to Mrs. Ochoa how Manuel's eyes zoned in on the forgotten classroom's squalid floor and never left throughout his account. He recalled asking Manuel how he got the bruises, to which he responded, "Evil suspended me."

He asked Manuel what he had done to warrant the suspension. Manuel said he got a perfect score on a test and his reward was being immediately sent to Evil's office. When he arrived, Evil ordered him to admit he cheated. Manuel pleaded with her, telling her he studied for weeks, reading book after book, and knew the answers, but she didn't believe him. She shouted in his face, calling him a liar, telling him no student was that smart, and no student was capable of perfection. In a moment of lost control, Manuel shouted back at Evil and told her she was only accusing him of cheating because *she* wasn't that smart, and *she* wasn't capable of perfection.

Evil picked up her phone, called the secretary, got the phone number for Manuel' parents and without even glancing at the desperately pleading student, dialed the number. After pleasantly saying hello, Evil verbally painted a picture of Manuel as an uncontrollable monster, a bane of existence within the school who was going to be suspended for five days. When she hung up the phone, Manuel, who was in a state of paralyzing terror, said the principal stared at him with a look he described as neither empty, nor unusual, but full, and normal.

"Manuel told me when he tried to leave the office he walked into the door because all he could see were his father's fists."

Francisco paused, shook his head, gritted his teeth and finished the story by telling Mrs. Ochoa what Manuel told him, "Just before I opened the door to leave, Evil told me my dad was furious and said he would make me pay for what I did. Then she started to laugh."

Francisco covered his mouth with his hand, exhaled loudly through his nose, removed his hand, and said, "She knew exactly what would happen to him, and she did it anyway, and then to laugh at him? How can somebody do that?"

His head sank and swayed from side to side, adding, "Manuel took off his shirt and showed me the bruises. They were everywhere, his arms, his back, his stomach. They were purple, blue, green, yellow. He told me he got new ones each day throughout his suspension, but never on the face, never where people could see them."

Mrs. Ochoa remained quiet. Francisco looked around. Throughout his whispered recap of Manuel's story, the next period's class filled up. Every desk was occupied. The noise level increased as chatter swept throughout the room.

"Francisco," Mrs. Ochoa said. "Did you want to keep discussing what you heard? You told me you finished seven interviews today, and you've only told me about two of them. Did you want to step out, so you can tell me about the other five?"

Francisco shook his head. Exasperated, he couldn't summon the strength to express what the other five students told him. He turned, glared at the seated students, turned back to the teacher and said, "Did you know these things were happening?"

The teacher nodded.

"How could you know these kinds of things were happening, and do nothing?"

Mrs. Ochoa lowered her head and replied, "I wish I could do something about it, Francisco, and as much as it sickens me, if I say anything, I'll lose my job, and I have a family of my own to worry about."

He was about to respond before Mrs. Ochoa looked up and added, "Did you want to spend this period doing more interviews?"

Following her question, there was a hopeful eagerness painted all over her face, but she remained quiet, anxiously awaiting his response.

"Yes," he replied.

He turned and walked out of the class. Standing in the main hallway, he looked to one side and then to the other. There were no more students stampeding through it, as they were all obediently seated at their desks in their designated classrooms. When he reached the door of the discarded, derelict classroom, he unlocked it with the small key kept safely in his pocket. He rotated the knob of the unlocked door, pushed it forward, passed through the doorway, turned on the light, sat down at the same dusty desk at the forefront of the musty smelling classroom and waited for his next sketch.

By the end of the period, eighteen fully formed sketches, all with their own unique stories and personalities, populated Francisco's brain. Each and every one of them desperately pleading for the opportunity to grace the face of the school's surrounding wall. When he returned to Mrs. Ochoa's classroom, he approached his mobile table filled with his cache of artistic materials and pushed it out of the room without saying a word.

"Good luck," Mrs. Ochoa said just before Francisco left the classroom.

Francisco didn't reply or break stride as he left the classroom. He didn't bother stopping at Mr. Ignacio's class to pick up any of the work he had absolutely no intention of doing anyway. He just went directly to the school's surrounding wall. Once there he started painting Gabriel's portrait steps away from the portrait of the disgruntled athlete he spoke to a day earlier. He was almost finished when he heard the bell signaling the start of the next period.

Gym class.

Perfect, he thought.

He continued painting. He was left undisturbed, as neither the students, nor the supply teacher cared to notice him, or what he was doing. Just as he finished the final touches needed to infuriate Gabriel's eyes with the scarlet tip of the smallest of his five brushes, the school's bell rang again.

Lunch.

His stomach grumbled, but as he stepped back and nodded at the figure of Gabriel, he took several steps to his right and started painting Carmen's portrait. After two hours, and two short rounds of bell ringing later, the second round indicating the end of the school day, he finished Carmen's portrait.

He heard the commotion of his fellow students leaving the school, but couldn't join them, as the sketch of Manuel, anxiously waiting his turn, squeezed Francisco's nerves in a fit of excitement at finally having the chance to taste freedom. He started to paint. After ten minutes, his wrist really started to ache. He paused and shook his hand in an effort to alleviate the strain and saw Mrs. Ochoa standing in the middle of the paved field.

"Francisco, what are you still doing here, shouldn't you be going hom—"

Her words were overtaken by a gasp of astonished air, as she approached, stood in front of and stared at the three full-bodied, life-size portraits Francisco had completed.

"Are they good?" he asked.

"They're incredible," she replied.

Nervous humility settled over Francisco's eyebrows.

"Thank-you," he said. "I wanted to keep painting. Manuel has been waiting all day, but—"

"Manuel is here with you?" Mrs. Ochoa interrupted.

He turned back to the wall, where only Manuel's spotless black shoes were visible.

"He will be soon."

Mrs. Ochoa got closer. Francisco turned and saw his favorite teacher lean over his shoulder, looking down at the shoes belonging to the still unpainted body of Manuel.

"What about your parents?" she questioned.

With conflicted indecision plaguing him, he replied, "My dad is coming to pick me up. He's probably already here, but I really want to keep working."

Mrs. Ochoa smiled, reached into her purse and pulled out a cellular phone.

"What is your father's phone number?"

His eyes brightened. He gave her the number. She dialed it before pressing the phone against her ear.

"Hello, Mr. Morelos? Hi, this is Mrs. Ochoa... Yes, I'm Francisco's art teacher... Yes, I've been helping him with the project he has to do. That's actually why I'm calling you... No, no, nothing is wrong."

She laughed.

"No, he's not in trouble. He's with me right now, painting... Oh, you're already here waiting for him?"

Francisco glared at the teacher with distress creasing the skin of his face.

"He really wanted to finish a portrait he was working on and... Yes, that would be perfect. Yes, I will tell him. Another two hours."

She looked at Francisco, who held up his hand, and out-stretched all five of his fingers.

"He asked me if five more hours is okay... Will I be here with him?"

Francisco counted three long seconds before Mrs. Ochoa said, "Yes I will. Perfect, yes I'll tell him that it's okay. Yes, it's no problem at all. Take care."

She laughed then said, "Yes, he is my best student, Mr. Morelos... Okay, I'll see you then."

She hung up the phone, returned it to her purse, and said, "Since I promised your dad that I'm going to be staying here for the next five hours, I might as well ask if you need anything?"

With a grand smile spreading across his face, Francisco said no.

"Okay, Victor, I'll be back in my office, catching up on some things. Bring back the table when you're finished, and don't lose track of time, you only have five more hours."

Francisco thanked her, repeatedly, asking her over and over if she was sure it was okay, that five hours was a long time, expressing concern about her family, to which she smiled and told him it was fine. He was about to return to his work, when Mrs. Ochoa gently placed her hand on his shoulder.

"I want you to have this," she said.

She handed him another key. It was nearly twice the length of the first key she gave him.

"You'll need it to get into my office because I have to keep the door locked after school hours."

Five hours later, Francisco took a step back and gazed at the portraits he had finished. All of them had raging red eyes and wide smiles laughing mightily.

Passing through the school's main hallway, Francisco marveled at the emptiness of the building. No students. No teachers. When he finally reached Mrs. Ochoa's classroom, he pushed the key she gave him into the doorknob. He heard a click, turned the knob and entered the room. His shoulders relaxed, his face softened, and a grin grew when he saw the teacher sleeping. Her face was nestled in the pillowed skin where her slim right forearm and small right bicep met. He pushed the table two steps before the teacher's head shot up. She rubbed her eyes and smiled.

He smiled back, pushed the table to the back of the class, and thanked Mrs. Ochoa again for her kindness. Together they walked out of the classroom and went down the school's main hallway.

"Your portraits are amazing, Francisco."

"Thanks," he replied. "I'm just worried I can't work on them after tomorrow because of the weekend."

Mrs. Ochoa reached into her purse and pulled out yet another key. It was slightly shorter than the last key she gave him, but longer than the first one. She handed it to him and said, "This key is for a door at the rear of the school, have you seen it?"

He said he hadn't.

"That's okay, nobody notices it, but it's there. Anyway, this key will get you in and out of the building so you can work after school hours and even on the weekends if you want, without anybody bothering you."

"Are you serious?" he said, his words barreling down both sides of the hallway, but left unheard by anybody but him and Mrs. Ochoa.

"Yes," the teacher replied.

He gazed at the key with reverence.

"Thank you so much."

Still refusing to believe such an opportunity could be possible, he put the key in his pocket, where it joined the other two keys she gave him. They started walking until, with fear halting him with an unforgiving grip, he said, "As much as it helps me being able to work extra days, won't I get in trouble for being here on the weekend? Won't Evil know I've been here when she sees more portraits on the wall when she arrives on Monday?"

"She won't care how you did it," Mrs. Ochoa said. "All she cares about is getting what she wants."

"What about the security guards?"

"Don't worry about them," she replied. "They're not around on weekends. They're not even around now. They leave as soon as the last student leaves."

"But I'm still here," he said.

"They're not the most dedicated people, Francisco."

After sharing a laugh, they both started walking again. When they reached the building's front door, Francisco rushed in front of the teacher and opened it for her. She thanked him and walked through the doorway. Francisco followed, and the first thing he noticed was the vacant booth where one of the two fat security guards always sat, ate and watched TV.

"I told you," Mrs. Ochoa said before shaking her head and adding, "I heard they won't even be around at all during the last week of school."

Francisco looked up. The sky had already begun to darken. He looked ahead and saw his father's car on the other side of the gate, parked and waiting.

"How do we get out through the locked gate?"

Mrs. Ochoa walked in front of him, pulled yet another key from her purse, effortlessly used it to open the gate and handed it to him. It was nearly identical in size and shape to the last key she gave him. He accepted it graciously.

"You need a lot keys to get through this place," he said.

"In this school," she said, "every door is locked."

8.

After leaving Evil's office, where he paid the principal everything he had saved over the last nine months for a pair of pants he'd yet to see, and doubted he ever would, Francisco made his way to Ms. Vasquez's classroom. Ms. Vasquez stood from behind her large, spotless desk and unveiled a livid sneer. She walked to a nearby cabinet, opened a drawer, pulled out a textbook identical to the one held in her other hand, returned to her desk and slammed it down. Indifferent to the roots of the teacher's ire, Francisco ignored the book she put in front of him and asked her if he could interview students for his project.

"*Absolutely not,*" she said, "I've heard about your *interviews*, Francisco. I've heard the whispers of your *subjects'* misplaced, misinformed lies. They are nothing but attempts at defacing Ms. Espinosa, who happens to be a dear friend of mine," as she glared at the portrait of the principal sitting on its mantel next to the clock and smiled.

Tearing her attention away from the portrait of Evil and ignoring Francisco, Ms. Vasquez blissfully opened her book, cradled the book in one arm, raised her other arm, extended her index finger and pointed at a student seated in the middle of the second row. The student was hidden behind a much taller student sitting in front of him. Nonetheless, Ms. Vasquez spotted him and ordered him to start reading aloud.

Glancing at an empty desk in the front row where Veronika used to sit, Francisco watched the chosen student turn his head away in a futile attempt at diverting the teacher's attention.

"Yes, I'm pointing at you," Ms. Vasquez said. "Stand up."

The student rose from his chair. He started to shake. He looked around the room frantically, cowering after noticing several sets of eyes staring back at him. He focused his attention on Ms. Vasquez and implored her to choose somebody else to do the reading. His voice was stricken, quivering as if he was begging the teacher to spare his life. Unmoved by his pleas, Ms. Vasquez repeated her order for him to read aloud.

"Start from the third paragraph on page one-hundred and twenty-two," she said.

The student looked around again, silently appealing for assistance Francisco knew was never going to come. The student flipped through the pages of the book and looked down at the page he was ordered to read. He opened his mouth, allowing a single subdued word to escape, before slamming his mouth shut.

"What was that?" Ms. Vasquez questioned. "You're going to have to speak up."

The trembling student raised his head, revealing a set of tortured eyes dampened with tears ready to slide down his pockmarked cheeks. A sketch started to form in Francisco's mind.

"Come on," Ms. Vasquez said. "I don't have all day."

Curious as to what the student was ordered to read, Francisco stepped to the teacher's desk, opened the book she initially laid out for him, flipped to the one-hundred and twenty-second page, skimmed down to the third paragraph and waited for the student to start. The student lowered his head once again, opened his mouth and muttered words neither Francisco, nor the teacher, nor anybody else in the room, could possibly hear.

"For the love of God," Ms. Vasquez said. *"Speak up."*

The student took a deep breath and recommenced his reading, this time speaking loud enough for everybody to hear.

"P... Pri... Prid..."

"The word is *Pride*," Ms. Vasquez said. "Something you clearly don't have."

The student raised his head. His face was vacant. Tears welled up in his eyes and trickled down his cheek. He wiped away the glistening droplets, looked back down and continued.

"In on... one... one's... cu .. cun... cun--"

"*Country*," Ms. Vasquez thundered out.

"Is an... int... int..."

"Jesus Christ," Ms. Vasquez said, "*Pride in one's country is an integral part of building a strong nation.*"

The student retreated back to his seat and buried his face in the book laid out before him. Over a few scattered chuckles from some of the other students in the room, all Francisco could hear was the humiliated student's whimpering. Ms. Vasquez, unmoved by the damage she had done, shook her head and laughed, faintly, but loud enough for Francisco to hear. She then started reading aloud from the point where the student faltered. Francisco ignored the teacher's words. His attention was focused on the shamed student, whose face remained obscured within the pages he could not read. He gazed at the student in an attempt to get a clear view of his face. The boy raised his head. Looking forward, he appeared to notice Francisco and stared at him, granting Francisco all the time he needed to sketch him in his mind. The student's eyes were red, not with fury however, but with grief. Francisco wanted to change that. After the student's head sank back down into his book, Francisco looked at the rest of the students, whose heads were also buried in their textbooks. He then looked back at Ms. Vasquez and started glaring at her fiercely.

When the bell rang, every student stood in unison and filed out of the classroom on their way to their next class. Francisco remained where he was, waiting, his feet firmly planted on the floor. As the students vacated the classroom, none of them looked at Ms. Vasquez or Francisco, except one, the disgraced student, who glanced at Francisco. All traces of the boy's past tears were gone, evaporated, as if they were never shed. After the student left the room, leaving nobody but Francisco and Ms. Vasquez, Francisco turned toward the teacher, who stood on the other side of her desk, her textbook still cradled in her arms.

"Francisco?" she said. "I didn't even know you were still here."

"Instead of embarrassing students who can't read," he said, why don't you try *teaching* them how to read?"

Ms. Vasquez dropped the textbook on her desk and approached him. He stood straight, staring back at her, blinking only when his body ordered him to.

"I suggest you focus on yourself, Francisco."

"I suggest you do your job," he replied.

"One more word," she said, "and I'll send you right back to Ms. Espinosa's office, and she'll deal with you."

"So somebody questions you and you just send them to Evil, just so she can ruin their life."

"What did you call her?" the teacher said.

"*Evil*" he replied. "Because that's what she is, and that's what you are. And there is no better word for people who hurt people the way you both do, and for people who *enjoy* hurting people the way you both do." But before Ms. Vasquez could respond, Francisco turned his back, approached the door, opened it and walked out of the classroom. Once he stepped outside, he was met by the humiliated student.

"Is it true you ask everybody in our grade what they hate about this school before you paint them?

Francisco nodded.

The student took a step forward and whispered, "I hate how this school is filled with books that I've never been taught to read."

The softness of the student's words only added to their anguish.

"Will that help you with my portrait?" the student asked. "I hope so because everybody in our grade is talking about how amazing your portraits are. We all can't wait to see our own on the surrounding wall."

"It does," Francisco replied. "It helps a lot. I'll do my best to make your portrait as good as I possibly can."

"And will mine have the same red eyes as the rest?" the student asked. "Will it be laughing like the rest of them, too?"

Francisco told the student his portrait would have the same red eyes and would be laughing like the rest, if that's what he wanted.

"It is," the student replied. "From what I've heard, it's what everybody in our grade wants."

"Then that's what I'll do," Francisco said.

The student's head sank, allowing Francisco to witness a stampede of students tearing through the hallway toward their next class, doubtlessly dreading the consequences of being late. When the student's head rose back up, he revealed a pained, but sincere smile.

"Thank you for that," the student said. "Thank you so much."

9.

Saturday arrived and Francisco woke up at the exact same time he did the day before. He rushed to his parent's bedroom, opened the door, took a step in, noticed both of them sleeping and knocked on the door until they woke up.

"What is it?" his father asked.

Already showered, dressed and fed, Francisco replied, "I need to go to school so I can work on my portraits."

His father, looking around the room as if he awoke in a place he didn't recognize, turned and whispered something to Francisco's mother, who responded with a smile. Looking back at his son, Francisco's father said, "You know it's Saturday, right?"

"Of course I do," Francisco said, "but I need to go, can you drive me?"

Francisco's father got out of bed and told his son to give him a few minutes, while Francisco's mother told him she would prepare him a lunch. When Francisco's father pulled up to the school, the sun settled in its seat, preparing to watch the world for another day. Francisco got out of the car, but before he closed the door, his father asked how he was going to get into the building, and if he was even allowed in. Francisco reached into his pocket and pulled out one of the four keys Mrs. Ochoa gave him, showed it to his father and told him his teacher said it would be all right for him to let himself in. Francisco's father nodded, Francisco shut the car door, and his father drove away.

With the gate key held firmly in his grasp, Francisco used it to pass through the school's front gate and then made his way into the building. When he reached Mrs. Ochoa's class, he used another one of the keys she gave him, unlocked the door and walked in. Awaiting him at the rear of the darkened room was his table and tools.

Once outside, alongside the wall, he worked obsessively throughout the day. He took a reluctant break only to eat the food his mother prepared for him when he could no longer concentrate as a result of the moans of his empty stomach. An hour after he ate his lunch, washing it down with a bottle of soda, he felt the wailing of his bladder. He tried to stave off the unnerving sensation of having to pee through sheer force of will, but it refused to be repressed. Not wishing to waste precious time wandering through the school's hallway in hopes of finding a washroom he assumed would have been locked anyway, and refusing to desecrate the surrounding wall that granted liberty to the students gracing its surface, Francisco darted to the school itself, and urinated along one of its many languid, concrete walls.

His father picked him up just as the sun, tired from its long shift, settled beneath the horizon. Francisco had completed eight portraits. Soon after he got home, he fell asleep not much later that evening.

The following day he awoke anxious to repeat his productivity, but it was not to be. His parents told him that they all had to attend church, and afterward they were going to spend the day with their extended family. Francisco begged for clemency from the event he knew was a once a week routine, but his parents were unwavering in their insistence he join them. They told him he needed a break from his work, a sentiment he vehemently refuted. Throughout the day, surrounded by those he was expected to love blindly, unconditionally, all he could think about were the students trapped in his mind, no longer pleading, but demanding to be let out and painted. As several members of his family droned on about things he cared nothing about, while gorging on a bottomless pit of food his parents provided for them, Francisco sat on the plastic chair, away from the crowd, where he did his best to quell the frenzied cries from the sketches stewing in his skull. He felt helpless to their cries, as the sketches had no choice but to remain dormant until they could finally be freed through the strokes of his paintbrushes.

The next day, Francisco worked furiously on an isolated section of the wall surrounding the school. When he heard footsteps stamping on the ground behind him, he turned, and standing there in front of him was a girl in the same grade as him, whose name he did not know. She smiled and complimented him on his latest portrait. The sun was bright, forcing him to shelter his eyes with one hand, while holding the smallest of the five brushes firmly in the other. The girl told him what she hated about the school without him even having to ask. She spilled out her sorrowful confession so rapidly he had to ask her to repeat herself. When she was finished, without any warning, she warmly wrapped her arms around him, thanked him, told him she couldn't wait to see her very own portrait on the wall and asked him if he could make her look as pretty as possible. He was about to tell the girl he would do the best he could, while knowing he would only paint her as he saw her, but was distracted by the sight of not one, not two, but four other students standing quietly behind her. They too were in the same grade as Francisco. All four of the students appeared eager to speak to him, and he had little doubt they were going to tell him the same kinds of stories as the girl who got to him first.

After hearing from all of the students who had lined up to reveal what they hated about the school, Francisco finished the portrait he'd already started. With the newly formed sketches all jostling for a position at the front of the line in his mind, he walked away from the wall, re-entered the school and walked through the main hallway in hopes not of clearing his head, but of organizing it, implementing order to the images populating it. He didn't get but a few steps in however, when another student in his grade rushed up to him and expressed what they hated about the school, followed by another, and another. Unsurprisingly, all of their spiteful, horrible stories revolved around Evil, and the abuses she unleashed, abuses that not only went unpunished, but garnered her awards, like the plaques hanging on the wall in her office. Francisco turned around. He couldn't hear any more of their stories for the day. He had to return to the wall. He had to return to work to let the ones in his head out before he could take any more in.

Passing through the door leading to his gym class, he walked through the field of pavement, but stopped when he noticed the supply teacher he was so used to seeing throughout the previous week was no longer there. He had been substituted by the teacher he was initially substituting for: Mr. Torres. Francisco immediately noticed a large bandage taped to the front of Mr. Torres' forehead. He made his way toward the gym teacher. Once he reached him, without saying hello, he asked what happened between him and Veronika.

"It's none of your concern," Mr. Torres said.

"Why do you have a bandage on your head?"

"It's none of your concern."

"You left the same time Veronika was suspended, and now you come back a week later with a big bandage on your head," Francisco said. "Something obviously happened, and I want to know what."

"It's none of your concern."

The sketches trapped in Francisco's head started to throttle the walls of his mind, screaming for their release, their anger enraged by the sound of Mr. Torres' voice. Students came out of the change rooms and huddled into a group in front of Mr. Torres, who turned toward them, ignoring Francisco, as if he wasn't even there. Knowing he was not going to receive any answers from the teacher as he started to blow his puny whistle after ordering the students standing before him to run five laps, Francisco turned and walked back toward the wall, where twenty-two portraits now resided. The only answers he was going to get about what happened to Veronika were going to have to come from Veronika herself, and he was going to have to wait another week for those.

He painted throughout the day, non-stop. He ignored the bells that rang every hour. Whenever an inconvenient itch made itself known, he disregarded it. Whenever he felt his mouth get dry, he licked his lips as a way to calm the strain of their parched surface. He silenced the grumbling of his famished stomach with deep breaths, as he worked tirelessly through his lunch break. When he finished a portrait, he didn't even bother looking at it. He just stepped aside and started working on the next one. As the end of the school day approached, he glanced at his watch. He had five minutes to return his arsenal back to Mrs. Ochoa's class and meet his father at the front gate of the school. The night before, his father told him he would pick him up at five o'clock, every day. He asked to be allowed to stay until eight o'clock just like he did when Mrs. Ochoa stayed with him, but his father insisted five o'clock was the latest he would allow his son to stay alone in the school. Francisco had reluctantly agreed.

He stepped away from the portraits, placing the smallest of the five brushes back on the table. He then pushed the table back into the school. After re-entering the building, he walked through the empty hallway until he reached his favorite teacher's classroom. Once inside, he looked around and focused on the portrait of Evil resting comfortably atop its wooden mantel.

With Evil gazing down at him, Francisco thought back to when he viewed her as an adversary, an imposing figure of opposition that justified his position of defiance, but after hearing more and more students' stories, his view changed. An adversary is often preceded by the word worthy, but there was nothing worthy about Evil. He felt nothing but contempt toward her, and believed she was worthy of nothing but shame and misery.

He grabbed the desk nearest to him, positioned it directly underneath the wooden mantel and stood on it, doing all he could to balance himself. Confident he wasn't going to topple over, Francisco stretched his arm out until he was able to grasp the finely framed portrait. It was heavy, the framing sturdy. The glass plate covering Evil's face was thick, shielding her in a well-crafted casing that didn't contain a single speck of dust.

Francisco spit on the portrait. His saliva slid down the glass shield like the tears he envisioned rolling down the cheeks of Evil's most degraded victims. He looked around. Certain that nobody else was around, he raised the portrait as high as he could, turned it around so he no longer had to stare at her face, and while still balancing himself on the rickety desk, he slammed the portrait against the wooden mantel.

The sound of the portrait's glass cracking was marvelous. He stared at the mangled pedestal with splendor. He turned the portrait over and saw several long gashes spread crookedly across her face, disfiguring it. He turned the picture back around, and with Evil seeing nothing but the wall, he placed it back on the ruined mantel, stepped down from the fragile desk, exited the classroom and made his way to his father's car, its engine humming calmly.

* * *

The following day, Francisco rushed to Mrs. Ochoa's class to get his table and supplies so he could get back to work. He didn't even bother going to Evil's office, or Ms. Vasquez's first period class. Once inside his favorite teacher's classroom, he was stunned when he looked up and saw, propped up on what appeared to be a perfectly restored wooden mantel, Evil's portrait brashly staring out at the class. All of the jagged scars he inflicted upon it the day before were gone, as if they were never suffered. He turned and glared at Mrs. Ochoa with a look of shaken perplexity.

"Francisco," the teacher said softly, "Why don't you step outside with me for a moment."

Without saying a word, he followed the teacher as she exited the room. Standing in the empty hallway, he was about to speak before Mrs. Ochoa put her index finger over her lips. Confused, he looked around and spotted one of the fat guards waddling down the hallway toward them, a giant bottle of soda held firmly in his bulbous hand.

"Let's go to the other classroom," she said quietly, "Do you still have the key?"

He nodded, while shifting his sight from Mrs. Ochoa to the fat guard sluggishly approaching. Once inside the classroom he used to conduct several of his interviews, Francisco flicked on the light and closed the door.

"What happened?" he said.

Mrs. Ochoa rested her hand on his shoulder and replied, "I had to pay for a new portrait and mantel."

"Why?"

"My class, my responsibility."

Without a second thought, without a moment's hesitation, Francisco told Mrs. Ochoa he broke the portrait and damaged the mantel, and he would take full responsibility for it. The teacher replied with a tender smile and told him she knew he was the one who committed what Evil considered an unforgivable crime.

"If you knew it was me, why didn't you say anything?" he said.

"I've had to look at that horribly perfect picture every single morning for as long as I've been teaching here, and I can't tell you how many times I've thought about doing what you did."

Francisco flashed a regrettable grin, before saying, "Yeah, but you had to pay for it."

"Some things are worth the price."

"It felt really good," he said.

"I noticed," Mrs. Ochoa replied, "I saw all the damage you did to it, and so did Evil. I don't think I've seen her that upset in a long, long time."

"But how did she see it? Aren't you the first one to come into your class? Aren't we the only ones who have a key?"

Mrs. Ochoa explained to Francisco that every single day Evil arrived at school before everybody else and inspected every classroom using a master key granting her unlimited access to anywhere she wanted.

"She says she does it to make sure the school is up to the high standards she set, but we all know she only does it to make sure her portraits are immaculately maintained."

Francisco asked Mrs. Ochoa if Evil had any suspicions as to who defaced her portrait.

"I just told her I left without locking the door, and somebody probably just walked in and did it, most likely a student who resented her."

Francisco laughed at how much truth could be found in a lie, but he started to panic and asked the teacher if it was possible that he was seen by a security camera or something else that would tie him to the crime.

"Don't worry," Mrs. Ochoa said.

"Are you sure?" he asked.

Mrs. Ochoa told him how a few months earlier, after a rash of kidnappings took place near another school in the south side of the city, many parents urged Evil to invest in security cameras to ensure the safety of their children. Evil refused, saying the expenditure was unnecessary as every student was perfectly safe under the watchful eyes of her well-trained, hard-working security staff. Mrs. Ochoa failed in her attempt to maintain a straight face at her last few words, but assured Francisco that where she failed, Evil succeeded.

Relieved, Francisco shook his head before catching a glimpse of a portrait of Evil resting on a mantel identical to the ones used in every other classroom in the school. He remembered noticing the portrait the first time he entered the dusty, abandoned classroom, just before his interview with Gabriel, but didn't notice how spotless it was. The disparity between its state and the condition of the rest of the neglected classroom was astounding. Noticing her student's shift in attention, Mrs. Ochoa said, "I have to clean the portrait in my class, and this class, every day, as soon as I come in."

Refocusing his attention to the teacher, Francisco asked how much she had to pay, and how everything got fixed so fast. Mrs. Ochoa explained to Francisco that behind Evil's desk were two drawers. In the first drawer were fresh new replacement portraits in the event of one of them being damaged, and in the second drawer were spotless, replacement mantels. As for the price, she told him it wasn't cheap, as Evil made the teachers she deemed responsible pay a little for the new materials, and a lot for the disrespect. Francisco apologized again, but Mrs. Ochoa brushed his apology aside, before asking him how his portraits were going.

"Good," he replied. "I'm going to spend all day today working on them."

"You have less than two weeks. How is your pace?"

He told her he hoped to finish his thirty-third portrait by the time his father picked him up at the end of the day. Mrs. Ochoa told him if he needed any help, she was there.

* * *

Over the next two days Francisco's steps followed in the exact same footprints he left behind the day before. The only change that took place over that short span of time was the size of the bandage pasted on Mr. Torres' forehead, which got smaller and smaller. When he walked into school on the Friday of the second to last week of classes, five minutes before the first period of the day was set to begin, Francisco went directly to Mrs. Ochoa's classroom, grabbed his table and wheeled it out of the room, pausing only to warmly greet his favorite teacher, who reciprocated the gesture tenderly. After he exited the classroom, he walked down the main hallway. All of those students who shared his grade started to draw upon him, swallowing him with their scorn, bombarding him with their confessions. Their once muted murmurs exploded in a riotous roar, as they shouted out what they hated about the school, and the Evil running it. Desperate to free himself from the suffocating grip of the students' dissent, he was about to cry out that he wanted to be left alone, until he realized without those students' vilifying declarations and their sorrowful stories, notwithstanding their superficial, petty requests, he would never be able to paint them with the perfection Evil demanded, and he would personally suffer because of it, so he stood silently in the center of the adolescent mob, rotating his head from side to side. He opened his ears, inhaled deeply, held his breath and did his best to snatch a story from every shout and snatch a sketch from every student.

In what seemed to be no time at all, there were enough sketches chomping at the bit to taste the freedom of the school's surrounding wall to keep him busy throughout the weekend and well into the following week. Realizing, reluctantly, there was no room left in his mind for more sketches without the fear of sacrificing those that already safely made it inside, he raised his arms, a gesture that astonishingly silenced the crowd, and said he had to return to his work. He added, without pre-planning the words, a promise that he would listen to, and paint, every single student who shared his grade. Though it was a promise he had to keep, as he had to paint every student in his grade anyway, it was a promise he now *wanted* to keep.

He grabbed the edges of the table and managed a single step before he felt the side of his body violently shoved against one of the school's rusted lockers. His first fear lay with the table he was torn away from. He shot a glance toward it, and despite the instant surge of pain throbbing throughout his upper body, he was relieved the fragile table and the supplies it housed were left unharmed. He turned his head. Standing before him were two older, bigger boys. He didn't recognize them. All he knew was they were not in his grade. He shifted his body. Now directly facing the two boys, he loudly questioned them as to why they were harassing him, hoping his shouted words would inspire the pack of students who shared his grade to interfere. But his peers just stood idly by. All of the energy they put forth while expressing their confessions was gone. Confident no resistance was to come, the two boys responded to Francisco's raised voice with wide smiles and denigrating laughter. One of the boys, the smaller of the two, stepped forward and told Francisco to stop riling people up. Francisco looked back at the group of apathetic students, all of whom stared back at him quietly and stupidly, while the sketches dwelling in his mind screamed, clawing at the walls, unleashing a fervent ardor. The sketches were clearly louder, stronger, more livid than the weak, silent students whose tales of woe birthed them. He returned his attention to the boy standing before him.

"Does anybody here look riled up to you?"

The second, larger of the two boys, who already had traces of a mustache growing above his upper lip, stepped in front of Francisco. The boy didn't say a word. He just shoved Francisco back against the same locker. The impact was loud and painful. Francisco grimaced and tried to exhale, but he was out of breath. He bent down in an effort to expedite his recovery. After finally recapturing the ability to breathe, he reinstated his upright posture, only to see the same two boys standing in front of him, the school's golden crest stitched on their shirts staring him in the face.

"Listen," the smaller of the two boys said, traces of his own mustache sprouting from the fertile skin above his upper lip, "summer vacation is less than two weeks away, so stop starting shit. Just keep quiet and do the stupid paintings."

Francisco looked up and met the eyes of the boy addressing him. He was about to respond. His mouth drew open, but stopped, when the second, larger boy drew upon him. Fearing what he believed was sure to occur if he said what he wanted to say, Francisco closed his mouth and stared at the floor. Then the bell rang. When he looked back up, the two boys were gone. He turned and saw them walking down the hallway. He turned back toward the area where the group of students who shared his grade stood and watched, but they had already dispersed, rushing to their classes. Francisco stepped away from the locker, turned around and saw a large dent in the spot where his back struck. He returned to his table. Standing on the other side of it was Mrs. Ochoa, who must have heard the commotion from her nearby classroom.

"Are you okay?" she said.

"I'm fine," he replied. "I don't know who they were, but you know even if I did, I couldn't tell you."

"Carlos and Ulises," she said.

"Like I said, I don't know who they were, and I'm not saying names. I know the rules of the school. Please, don't do anything. It was nothing."

Mrs. Ochoa walked around the table and placed her hand on his shoulder. He tried to subdue the shaking of his body, fearing she would feel it, ignore his requests and end up hurting him even more in a foolhardy attempt to help him.

"Don't worry," she said. "I won't say anything. I promise. If anything, saying something would just get me in trouble."

Confused, he questioned her as to how that was possible.

"They're Evil's nephews."

Francisco didn't say anything. He didn't have to. He just shook his head and laughed. Mrs. Ochoa didn't elaborate. She didn't have to either. She just shook her head and laughed as well.

After his favorite teacher left and returned to her classroom, Francisco went to the paved field. He spotted Mr. Torres and noticed the bandage on his head was now gone, and the only visible proof of his mysterious injury was a small, barely discernible scar. Without even glancing at the portraits he had already completed, Francisco found a vacant area on the wall and immediately got to work. He painted frenetically, but precisely. Armed with his brushes and multiple mixtures of paint, he captured every detail his mind absorbed from the sketched students who fervently petitioned for liberty.

The sun was sluggish, preferring the cover of clouds throughout the morning. During a moment of clarity, the sun shined bright and breathed life into a shadow that cast its presence upon Francisco's latest mural. The portrait had no choice but to endure the shadow's swathe, for it was stuck where it was, unable to avoid the shroud of darkness. The shadow resembled a living figure made entirely of thick, woven strands of smoke. Faceless, it had no expression. Silent, it loomed ominously. Hesitant to turn and identify the source of the murky figure, Francisco continued scrutinizing it as it engulfed the portrait, draining the radiance he worked so hard to stimulate.

He tried to establish an identity for the shadow, but was unable to do so, as the rounded figure resembled nobody and everybody. The bell rang. The sound shook Francisco, causing him to drop the smallest of his five brushes. Small drops of red paint he just finished using to fill his current portrait's eyes splashed on the ground and seeped into the pavement. He knelt down, picked up the smallest tool in his cache and felt a hand on his shoulder. He didn't look back, but forward, directly at the shadow, while the laughing portrait, consumed by the shadow's gloomy cloak, stared back at him. The hand squeezed his shoulder, but not a word was spoken. He took a deep breath. His entire upper body expanded, but the hand refused to relinquish its grip. He felt nails pressing against his skin.

"Very good," the figure standing behind Francisco said, the shadow it spawned remaining silent.

The voice was familiar, regrettably so, and Francisco, feeling the blood in his body streaming powerfully through his veins, reinvigorating his muscles, stood and turned. Facing him, glaring up into his eyes was the source of the shadow, the principal, Evil Espinosa.

"I love how perfectly you painted the student's uniform," she said, "particularly the school's crest."

He didn't respond, offering nothing more than a disingenuous breath through his flaring nostrils.

"I swear it looks like it could jump off the wall," she said, "and such lovely smiles as well. Those were a nice touch."

Frustrated that the principal continued hovering and talking, maddeningly preventing him from continuing his work, Francisco just nodded, hoping his lack of a verbal response would hasten her departure. Evil, dismissing his hint, continued her barrage of compliments. Her flattery covered the entirety of the portrait, yet strangely neglected the figure's fuming, red eyes glaring back at her hatefully. Finally satisfied she said enough, the principal turned her back and walked away. *Fifty-one done, forty-one left,* he told himself.

He grabbed the largest of the five brushes, dipped the bristles into one of the mixtures pooled in the flimsy, plastic tray, chose one of the sketches crowding his mind and was about to start portrait number fifty-two, when his hand sank and fell to his side. Tears of paint fell from the tips of the brush's mane. He stared at the blank section of the wall, his canvas, a limitless universe. Having passed the halfway point of the ninety-two students he was ordered to paint, with the weekend coming up, along with only five more school days, he wondered if he would be able to finish on time. He also wondered if some of the students he spoke to, with all their cowardice, their superficiality, their weakness, their stupidity, were even worth the effort, worth the time, worth the pain, worth the paint. He shut his eyes, but only for a moment, and when he opened them, he got back to work, realizing that while not all of the students were deserving of the portraits he created, the sketches, the spirits of those students, all deserved to be freed from his head.

* * *

On both Saturday *and* Sunday, as he was granted a surprising leave of absence from spending the second day of the weekend with his family after an impassioned appeal the night before, Francisco woke up dark and early. Each day he showered, ate breakfast, grabbed a bag filled with a lunch his mother prepared for him and made sure he had all of the keys Mrs. Ochoa had given him. After his father dropped him off at school, he got his supplies and got to work. His wrist and eyes repudiated any pain or strain they felt throughout those days, while his strokes were strong and true.

Even though he was focused on the release of the sketches from his mind for the duration of the weekend's work, he couldn't help but think about Veronika, whose fast approaching return to school filled him with excitement. He couldn't wait to find out what happened between her and Mr. Torres. He couldn't wait to show her every single portrait he painted, all sixty-four of them, but most of all, he couldn't wait to finally see her pretty face again.

10.

On Monday, Francisco jumped out of bed, showered, ate, grabbed his lunch and got into the passenger seat of his father's car. Amidst a dissipating drizzle, he sat impatiently while the car trudged through the awakening city on the way to school. Upon arriving, as soon as the car came to a stop, he thanked his father and darted out of the vehicle before his father was able to respond. As if being chased, he dashed through the school's opened front gate, passing the empty security booth. Once inside the building, he hurried through the main hallway, reached the door of the classroom he wished to enter, heard the bell ring and opened it. Inside the classroom, his attention was captured by a flickering light above, near the rear of the room, the same one he imagined two weeks earlier crashing down and striking the good looking student seated beneath it. When he looked down however, the handsome youth, whom he had interviewed five days earlier and had provided a rather tame response to the question of what he hated about the school, was not there. Dismissing the vacancy, Francisco scanned the rest of the occupied desks until he found who he was looking for, and there she was, smiling at him. All of Veronika's features remained the same, but as a result of the suspended time, they appeared different, as if he was seeing them for the first time.

"Will you come with me outside?" he asked.

Before she could speak, Ms. Vasquez shouted, "Francisco, what do you think you're doing?"

With his eyes never leaving Veronika's face, he said, "I was going outside, to the wall, and I wanted to know if Veronika would come with me."

"And what makes you think I would allow her to leave with you?" the teacher countered.

"She's in the same grade as me," he replied.

"And why does that matter?"

After a moment, she continued, "Well, Francisco? Tell me, why does her grade matter?"

Francisco turned to her.

"Am I talking to myself here? Hello? I'm waiting. Are you unable to speak? I would like an answer. Vic--"

"Shut up," he said, cutting her off.

There was a collective gasp from the students inside the classroom, while Francisco, whose attention returned to Veronika, stood nervously, awaiting a response, not from Ms. Vasquez, whose reply meant nothing to him, but from Veronika, whose reply meant everything to him. Veronika opened her mouth, but her voice was once again impeded by Ms. Vasquez, who angrily demanded that Francisco explain and apologize for his rudeness. Francisco turned to Ms. Vasquez, a gesture that only intensified his already teeming aggravation, as he was no longer able to gaze at the girl he yearned to see for the duration of her suspension.

"Evil, I'm sorry, *Ms. Espinosa,* made it very clear to me that I had to paint every single student in my grade," he said. "Veronika is in my grade, and I haven't painted her yet, so if you have a problem with that, take it up with your *dear friend.*"

He turned back to Veronika.

"So, will you come with me?"

Veronika, already thwarted by Ms. Vasquez on two occasions, gathered her books, stuffed them in her knapsack, slung the bag over her shoulder, approached the door leading out of the classroom, wrapped her hand around the door knob, glanced at Francisco, smiled and gestured for him to join her. With Ms. Vasquez standing silent, Francisco rushed to the door, and in seconds was by Veronika's side. She opened the door and stepped out. Without saying a word to the teacher, Francisco followed, the slamming of the door speaking for him.

For the duration of the journey down the school's main hallway that included a brief detour at Mrs. Ochoa's empty classroom where he rounded up his arsenal, Francisco sketched Veronika in his mind. She often glanced at him, offering him smile after smile, each one more enriching than the last. Once they reached the doorway leading to the school's surrounding wall that was adjacent to Mr. Torres' office, Veronika's facial expression shifted. Her smile disappeared. Her eyes slanted. She started breathing rapidly. She turned to Francisco. He asked what was wrong.

"Can we go through a different door?" she asked.

Without waiting a beat, he turned and walked the other way, pushing the table in front of him. Veronika followed, and they walked without speaking until they reached another door that would lead them outside. There they were met with a fresh, damp breeze. When Francisco glanced at Veronika, he noticed how the moisture of the air made her face glisten. Once outside, he told Veronika they had to walk for a few minutes before reaching the section of the wall where his last portrait was completed. She smiled, appearing to have completely forgotten about whatever it was that made her so uncomfortable less than a minute earlier. Several of the completed portraits were in view. Veronika turned to Francisco and said, "They're amazing. Can I touch them?"

"Of course," he replied.

She rushed to the wall. She ran along its side and brushed her fingers against the bodies and faces of every liberated mural. She returned and said, "These are the most amazing things I've ever seen. They look so real. How were you able to make them look so alive?"

Francisco explained his process to her, detailing the notebook Mrs. Ochoa gave him, how he asked students in their grade what they hated about the school, how his mind flooded with sketches that over time fused their fury with his own growing anger, feeding it, forcing him to paint rapidly just to make room for more. He told her, without getting into specifics, how horrible some of the stories were, how shameful the abuses some of the students endured, and how worthy Evil was of her nickname. He told her how after hearing so many stories he grew exhausted with indignation, but regardless of the weariness he felt, he continued painting, during school, after school, on the weekends, releasing each and every student whose enraged sketch screamed for the chance to stand without worry along the endless plane of the school's surrounding wall, where they were free to stare back at Evil with blazing red eyes and wide smiles laughing in her face. Quietly listening to Francisco's recap of the work he'd done, Veronika gazed at him before asking him how many interviews he had left to do.

"One."

"Who?"

"You."

She took a nervous step back.

"You want to interview me? Why?"

Bewildered by her anxiety, he approached her. She rebuked his effort with another step back and said, "You don't have to interview me. What I hate about this school doesn't matter."

"Of course it matters," he replied. "It's the only way I'll be able to paint you like the other portraits."

She turned away, but before he was able to say anything further, she turned back toward him. Her face was flush with fear, as if she was being threatened by a voice only she could hear.

"Are you okay?" he asked.

She didn't reply. Her head sank. She raised her hands and covered her face with her palms, the sound of her weeping leaking through her fingers. "I want to be free like they are." She said in a muffled voice before lowering her hands, raising her head, turning her body and pointing at the portraits on the wall. With her back still turned, Francisco remained quiet. He was unsure what to say, unsure how to console her, so he just stood there. "Their eyes," she said, "they're so powerful."

He approached the mobile table, knelt down and popped open the can of red paint using the metal thumb he'd used so many times before. The can was already half-empty, as its ardent color was not only required to fuel the fury in the eyes of the murals, but was also crucial in creating the brown hue of their skin. Nonetheless, he was confident there was still enough red paint to finish every portrait he had left to complete. He opened the rest of the cans and mixed several colors in the plastic tray, rarely looking down, as the process had become second nature and instinctive to him. Meanwhile, Veronika, whose back remained turned, continued staring at the wall, sporadically complimenting the painted figures, flattering them as if they could hear her words. She turned, and for a fleeting moment, Francisco swore her eyes were as scorching as those he painted on the faces of his portraits.

"My chest," she said. "What I hate about this school is my chest, and how everybody stares at it."

Thinking back to when she saved his life with a bottle of water two weeks earlier, only to have him return the favor by staring at the chest she just said she hated, filled him with shame.

"I'm so sorr—"

"Do you remember when I was going to have lunch with you that day after gym class," she said, interrupting his attempted apology, "but Mr. Torres wanted to see me first?"

"Yes."

"I know you were probably wondering why I never showed up."

Francisco didn't reply, afraid that he might say something that would stop her from finally telling him what he had been waiting so long to find out.

"When I went into his office, he locked the door and told me he saw you and me talking. He told me he could tell you liked me. Then he told me you had to pay for embarrassing him in front of everybody, and as he said that he was staring at my chest."

Veronika continued her story by detailing how Mr. Torres came at her, his hands outstretched, aimed at her young breasts. She said how once he got hold of her he fondled her while clasping her body close to his. She told Francisco how she cried out, yelling for the teacher to stop, to let her go, but nobody heard, nobody came and he didn't care. She went quiet, her face falling. Tears splashed against the pavement below, seeping into it.

"I'm sorry," she said.

"No," he replied. "It's not your fault. I just can't--"

He rushed toward her and wrapped his arms around her, but released his grip when he felt her squirming with the kind of panic that made him feel as if he were asphyxiating her. He stepped back and apologized over and over. She pointed at the portraits. "They don't feel anything, Francisco, no fear, no shame, no pain. They're invincible."

Desperate to change the subject, but knowing he couldn't, Francisco instead chose to bring up another aspect of it. "What happened to Ortiz's head?"

Veronika took a deep breath, and as if all the anguish she'd just expressed had vanished, she said, "I hit him with one of his trophies after he let me go." She explained how he crashed to the ground, blood spilling from a gash in his skull. She didn't show a single sign of pride for her actions however. Instead, her face was filled with regret.

"What happened after that?" Francisco felt ashamed for not only asking her to elaborate, but doing it so quickly and with such enthusiasm.

Remaining where she was, barely moving a muscle, except for the ones powering her jaw, Veronika, exhibiting no offense at Francisco's zeal, explained how Mr. Torres, who wrapped his bleeding head with a towel, told her she would be sorry for what she did. He then grabbed her by the arm and took her to Ms. Espinosa's office. She described the walk as torturous, that Mr. Torres, whose grip on her arm was fierce, insistently jerked it every few strides. Once inside the office, she detailed how the principal looked at the injured Mr. Torres and acted in a way she had never imagined possible, let alone seen, as the wretched woman rushed to his side and gently guided him into one of the chairs in front of her desk. Shaking her head as she spoke, Veronika told Francisco how she stood in a state of shock watching the principal, the vilest creature she'd ever encountered, soothe Mr. Torres by telling him she would give him paid time off, as much as he needed, and how she knelt down in front of him and compassionately questioned him as to what happened, and how he responded by pointing at Veronika. Seated on the second vacant chair in front of the principal's enormous black desk, ready to fall over in disbelief at how genuinely concerned Ms. Espinosa appeared, the principal turned to her, and in a terrifying voice told her she'd be sorry.

"It was as if she completely transformed," Veronika said, "but she didn't change into something else, she just changed back into herself."

She told Francisco how Ms. Espinosa, in front of Mr. Torres, who remained in his seat clutching the blood soaked towel against his injured head, got so close to her she could smell her awful breath. She continued by telling Francisco how the principal told her she would be suspended longer than any other student before her, and before she was able to voice any rebuttal, Ms. Espinosa also informed her she would be responsible for all of Mr. Torres' medical bills.

Francisco huffed out a breath of disgust, while Veronika, pausing to blow out a transparent cloud of dejection, looked at him, shook her head and continued. "I got up from the chair, but she grabbed my shoulders and squeezed them, hard, and sat me back down, her nails digging right into me."

Veronika explained how the principal told her if she didn't pay all of the medical bills, as well as take the blame for injuring Mr. Torres, she would be expelled from school and all the fees her parents paid for the following year would be forfeited. "She told me she would do everything in her power to make sure I didn't get into any another school in the city. She told me she had a lot of friends in other schools, so no matter what I decided to do I would pay."

"What did you say after that?" Francisco said.

"I got angry. I told her what Mr. Torres did to me, but she didn't care. She just stood there with her arms crossed. She told me he would never do something like that. She told me I made the whole thing up, that it never happened, and I was lucky she didn't turn me over to the police for assaulting a teacher."

Veronika's words were not spoken, but lashed out.

Barely able to contain his rage, Francisco turned away from Veronika, who continued her story by telling him as Ms. Espinosa was explaining to her everything that *didn't* happen, Mr. Torres was staring at her chest, smiling.

"After I saw that, I didn't say anything, I just sat there. What else could I say? What else could I do? After that, Evil told me to get out of her office. She said she didn't want to see me until the last week of school, and a bill for Mr. Torres' hospital fees would be sent to my house, and that it better be paid."

With his back still turned, Francisco asked, "Did your parents end up paying the bill?"

"Yes," she replied. "I told them I injured a teacher by accident, and when the bill came a few days later, they told me they only had enough money to either pay for the summer vacation they've been planning, or Mr. Torres's medical bill."

Veronika stopped, and though Francisco couldn't see it, he heard her sob. Before he could ask, she answered, "They paid the medical bill," adding, "If I told them the truth, who knows what could've happened. Who knows what Evil would have done? What if she got angry and kicked me out of school anyway, just for telling my parents? They would have still lost the money for tuition. There still wouldn't be a summer vacation. My dad would lose his job because we would have to move because Evil wouldn't have let me get into another school in the city. I also couldn't imagine telling my parents what Mr. Torres did to me. It was just easier to get it done and over with. What else could I do?"

Francisco wanted to turn around, hug Veronika and tell her everything was all right, but he couldn't. He wanted to tell her there was something he could do for her, but there wasn't. He was scared to see Veronika's face, scared to see the changes he believed were unavoidable, scared to witness the disappearance, the destruction, the death of her beauty, scared to look in her eyes and see the sadness he heard in her voice. But he couldn't close his eyes either. He was too scared her sketch, eager to be freed, would be changed as well. With his head sunken and despondent, he heard her approach. His entire body tensed when he felt her hands grasp his shoulder. She attempted to spin him around, but he resisted. Eventually, after several more attempts, he relented. He turned around, but his head remained lowered. Veronika gently placed her hand on his cheek. It was smooth and soft in the most beautiful way. She raised his head until they both stared at each other, eye to eye. Not only did her beauty remain intact, it appeared even more radiant and powerful than before. She smiled, and Francisco, amidst his sadness and rage, smiled back.

"Do you think you can still paint me?" she asked.

Without responding he approached his mobile table, grabbed the largest of his five brushes and got to work. He painted frantically. The speed from which he worked was remarkable.

Never had he painted so fast. And as Veronika's portrait came to life, he glanced back and saw her standing behind him, staring at her laughing reflection. In what seemed to be no time at all, he was finished, save one final detail. He walked to the table, grabbed the smallest of his five brushes and was about to dip its tip into a small pool of red paint, when she asked him to wait.

"You don't want me to paint your eyes?" he questioned.

"I do," she replied, "but I wanted to take a minute to look at it before you did."

"I can paint the eyes a different color if you want."

"No," she said. "I want you to paint me exactly like you painted them. Free me like you freed them."

"Are you sure?"

"Yes."

He lowered the small brush, but just before its bristles soaked in the red paint, Veronika, who continued staring at her portrait, asked him about Mr. Torres, about the wound she had inflicted on him. As he filled the eyes of Veronika's mural with the same red paint he used to fill the eyes of every other portrait, Francisco told her when Mr. Torres returned, there was a bandage on his head, but throughout the week, day after day, the bandage got smaller until it was gone, and that all that was left was a small, barely noticeable scar.

11.

The next morning, an elderly woman draped in a familiar yellow and green uniform handed Francisco's father a newspaper through the driver's side window of his car. Francisco watched his father reading the front page, shaking his head the entire time.

"What's wrong?"

"Nothing," his father replied before folding the newspaper and placing it between his and the passenger's seat, "don't worry about it."

The streetlight turned green. His father pushed the gas pedal, but had to abruptly brake when a car cut him off while making a tight right turn. The newspaper fell forward and unfolded. Francisco looked down and saw the newspaper's horrifying cover image of a person's bloodied, naked body and what was once a face. There weren't even a set of eyes remaining. There was nothing left but a burgundy colored skull with flayed flesh clinging to the contours.

It was a common occurrence to see a graphically depicted corpse on the front page of the city's most popular newspaper, and as per usual, the image was accompanied by a similarly sized photo of a young woman in a bikini, posing and smiling, but when Francisco looked closer, he saw, just below the pictures of the mutilated body and the posing woman, a much smaller picture of a police officer holding up a shirt. While the shirt was drenched with blood, Francisco was able to recognize a golden crest stitched on the front of it, the same golden crest stitched on his own shirt.

He leaned forward and picked up the newspaper. He didn't yet recognize who the victim was, since there was no face to identify, but he was certain the victim was a student in his school. He lowered his line of sight in hopes of ascertaining more information. Directly below the photograph were several lines of text.

THE BODY OF JOSÉ JIMENEZ ESCUTIA, AGED FIFTEEN, WAS FOUND THIS MORNING IN AN ALLEY NOT FAR FROM THE SCHOOL HE ATTENDED. THE BOY WAS KIDNAPPED YESTERDAY AFTERNOON, STEPS FROM THE SCHOOL'S FRONT ENTRANCE. THERE WERE NO WITNESSES AND NO SECURITY GUARDS ON HAND. DESPITE THE REQUESTED RANSOM BEING PAID, THE PERPETRATORS KILLED THE BOY ANYWAY. AUTHORITIES BELIEVE THE PURPOSE OF THE FACIAL MUTILATION WAS TO DELAY IDENTIFICATION OF THE VICTIM. POLICE WERE ABLE TO IDENTIFY THE VICTIM AFTER FINDING HIS BLOODSOAKED SCHOOL UNIFORM IN A DUMPSTER THREE BLOCKS AWAY FROM THE SCENE.

Francisco dropped the paper into his lap and stared straight ahead. He didn't blink for several seconds. All of the cars zooming in front of him clumped together in a giant floating blur. He glanced back down at the gruesome photograph, recalling exactly who the victim was and where he remembered him from.

José Jimenez Escutia was the good looking boy seated beneath the flickering light at the back of Ms. Vasquez's history class, the same boy Francisco imagined the light fixture falling on weeks earlier, the same boy who wasn't sitting at his desk the morning before. Francisco briefly imagined what kind of torture José was experiencing while he was staring at his desk, casually dismissing his absence, but set aside the thought, fearing if he clung to it too long, it would haunt him with grief.

After his father pulled up to the school, without saying good-bye, Francisco got out of the car and rushed toward the school, clutching the newspaper in his hand until his knuckles glowed white. Making his way toward the school's front gate, he stopped and stared at the security booth that was just as empty as it was the day before. He walked inside the building. He was shocked at how casually the students jostled and joked with each other as if it didn't matter that one of their own had been snatched, murdered and left in a bloody heap in a nearby alley, where even the acidic droplets from an overnight downpour were unable to wash away the blood left on his body and uniform.

Francisco walked into Ms. Vasquez's class, and the first thing he looked at, the first thing his attention fixated on, was the vacant desk below the flickering light fixture. He turned away from the desk he believed would forever remain empty, no matter who sat there, and saw Veronika. She flashed a smile he was unable to reciprocate. Her smile disappeared and was replaced by an expression of concern. He walked toward her, ignoring Ms. Vasquez, hearing the teacher's voice, but not listening to what she was saying. He placed the newspaper on Veronika's desk. Her face went flush then pale. She looked up at Francisco, but before she could speak, he told her to read the text scribed below José's photo. After she read it, Veronika spun around and stared at the vacant desk at the rear of the classroom. As she turned back around, her mouth drew open, but instead of hearing the sound of her soft voice, Francisco heard Ms. Vasquez's bitter speech behind him. His face clenched as he turned. Ms. Vasquez leaned forward and grabbed the paper. Without reading it, and barely glancing at the large, grisly photo of her own murdered student, she rolled up the paper and said, "Francisco, how dare you bring something so disturbing into my class. Nobody wants to see that. Nobody *needs* to see that."

She approached the garbage can beside her desk. She did not drop, nor toss, but whipped the newspaper inside the receptacle, making sure it sunk deep amidst the trash, never to be seen, never to escape. Francisco took a step back and stumbled, bumping into Veronika's desk. He turned and was about to offer an apology when he realized she wouldn't have heard it, as her head was sunken into her opened palms, weeping over the death of her classmate. With scorn scorching his face, Francisco turned to Ms. Vasquez, and without uttering a word, he stepped around her, knelt down and thrust his hand into the garbage can. He dug deep, sifting through the trash until he spotted a corner of the desecrated newspaper. With the newspaper in hand, he stood, walked toward the door, turned the knob and opened it angrily, slamming it against the wall. The noise did not ask, but demanded the attention of everybody inside the classroom, from Ms. Vasquez, whose face was twisted with aggravation, to Veronika, whose face rose from her palms, her eyes red with grief, to the rest of the students, whose faces were riddled with curious confusion.

"*Get Out,*" Ms. Vasquez barked.

"*Go to hell,*" Francisco replied.

The teacher's face exploded with rage, but before a single word of reprisal could be fired back at him, Francisco grabbed the door and shut it with a violent, unruly slam. He made his way toward Evil's office. There were no imaginative visions of water fountains, no playful schemes on how to steal a sip of soda from the secretary's bottle and no stealthy maneuvers carried out to avoid the security guards, for there were no longer any guards to be avoided. Once he reached the main office, Francisco ignored the frenetically typing, nameless secretary, who ignored him in kind. He effortlessly opened the large, heavy door of Evil's office. The pleasant aroma of Evil's perfumed chamber stung his nostrils. Shuffling through several papers, the principal looked up.

"Francisco," she said, barely making eye contact, "I hope the portraits I requested are almost finished."

He thrust his hand forward and slammed the newspaper on her desk. The impact created a mighty wind that swept the papers

Evil was sifting through right off her desk and on to the floor. The newspaper opened before her. She glanced at the gruesome image in the center of the front page and showed no reaction when she looked back up. Francisco was surprised, not at Evil's lack of reaction, but at his own surprise for being surprised at her lack of reaction.

"Why are you showing me a picture of a woman in a bikini?" she asked.

"*What?*" Francisco said, "Are you serious? I don't care about that picture. I care about the picture staring you in the face. The picture of the dead student. He was in my class, in my grade."

She looked back down at the newspaper's front page for a moment then looked back up, her face still devoid of any emotional reaction to what she had just seen."

"Yes, I found out about this early this morning. It's a tragedy, truly sad."

"You got rid of the security guards," he said. "If they were there, José would be alive. This is *your* fault."

Evil's face changed, suddenly encompassing that which inspired her name. Francisco took a step back, and was immediately ashamed of doing so.

"How dare you accuse me of these crimes?" she responded, showing infinitely more emotion at the accusation of being responsible for the gruesome image than at the gruesome nature of the image itself.

"How dare *you?*" he fired back. "How dare *you* risk our lives?"

Evil leaned back in her throne. Her face calmed. "I'm not going to get into this with you," she said. "I'm tired."

"*You're tired?*"

"Listen, it's good that you care so much about your fellow student. It's good that you're grieving his loss, but now you need to accept reality. He's gone, and the school has to keep advancing."

"*Advancing?*"

"Yes," she said, her eyes zeroing in on him. "Have you paint-ed his portrait yet?"

Francisco said no.

"Good, it's best you don't. The last thing we want to do is disrespect his memory."

"How would painting him be disrespecting his memory?" Francisco said. "Wouldn't a portrait of him be honoring his memory?"

Evil grabbed the newspaper. Handling it roughly, with the sounds of its crinkled pages stinging Francisco's nerves, she turned the paper around and held it up, forcing him to gaze at the photo of his murdered classmate. He turned away.

"Look at it."

"No."

"Exactly," she said. "Nobody wants to see that. Nobody wants to live with a horrific image like that in their heads, and that's why painting him would be a mistake. Look at it this way, Francisco; it's one less portrait to paint. It's less work for you and peaceful rest for him. Everybody wins." She placed the paper on her desk, face down. "Now, is there anything else?"

There was so much Francisco wished to say, but he couldn't find the words. They were too far down in his throat, stuck, too deep to capture, let alone utter.

"Well then," Evil said, "do me a favor before you leave and pick up the papers you were responsible for dropping."

In a daze, still attempting to make sense of everything he'd been told, he picked up the paper spread out on the spotless floor. Neatly grouped together, he placed the sheets on the corner of Evil's desk.

"Now you can go," she said.

He extended his hand toward the newspaper, but just before he felt the coarse edge of the front page, the principal pulled the paper away, nearly slicing his fingertips in the process.

"Like I said, Francisco, nobody wants to see this. Remember, it's about respecting poor--" She paused and glanced down at the newspaper's front page, "José's memory."

Without responding, Francisco turned around, grabbed the doorknob and pulled the door open. He was shocked at the door's reinvigorated heaviness. He stepped through the doorway, and as the door shut behind him, he heard the unmistakable sound of the newspaper striking the bottom of Evil's garbage can.

Walking through the hallway, Francisco closed his eyes, hoping to retrieve a sketch he knew resided somewhere deep in his mind. It took a few moments, but he saw it. Maimed and disfigured, it was ruined, and as it got larger, it started to scare him. He opened his eyes. He looked around intensely as if it were the first time he'd ever been inside the school. With his bearings restored, he continued down the hallway. Standing outside Mrs. Ochoa's classroom, Francisco opened the door. Filled with students staring at him curiously, he walked to the teacher's desk, knelt toward her and whispered a request to speak to her outside. She immediately rose and followed him out of the room, the students' collective gaze following them. Once outside, he asked Mrs. Ochoa if she'd heard about José. Her pained expression told him she had. He proceeded to tell her how Evil told him not to paint the murdered boy, that it would disrespect his memory.

"What do you want to do?" she asked.

"I want to paint him," he replied. "I think *not* painting him would disrespect his memory because it would be like he never existed."

"Then you know what you have to do."

"There's a problem, though," he said.

"What?"

He closed his eyes again, only to open them a moment later, his face fearful and flustered.

"The sketch I had of José. The one I drew in my head when I interviewed him last week is gone. All I can see now is the picture in the newspaper, and I don't want to paint him that way."

Mrs. Ochoa said she had an idea, and asked him to wait there while she went to the classroom to get something. Francisco stood in the hall, opening and closing his eyes in a desperate attempt to re-acquire the original sketch he now believed was as dead as the student who inspired it. He was unsuccessful, as he could no longer see the student for who he was, but only for what had been done to him. Mrs. Ochoa returned holding a hard covered book. She opened it. It was filled with photos, class pictures from the year before. She flipped through the pages until settling on a specific photo. She scanned the page with her finger until she found what she'd been looking for. Seated in the first of three rows of posing students, a smile spread across his youthful, handsome face was José Escutia.

"I know it's not a big photo, but would it help?"

Francisco stared at the photograph, absorbing the image.

"Francisco?"

He looked up and closed his eyes. Replacing the brutalized image of José's body from the newspaper was the handsome boy smiling from the photo he had just seen, and in seconds the grinning image became a beautiful sketch. He opened his eyes, smiled and thanked her.

"Do you need the book?" she asked.

"No," he said. "I have all I need."

She closed the book and asked him if he needed anything else. He said no. She asked him what he was going to do.

"Paint," he said. "I have more portraits to do and only a few days left to do them."

"And José?"

"I'm going to save the best for last."

Throughout the day, Francisco painted feverishly, his only interruption coming from Evil, just before lunch, which he dutifully skipped. She walked up behind him to check his progress. Angered at the loss of time, and even more angered at having it snatched away by Evil, he stared at her contemptuously as she asked him probing questions about who he was painting, and who he planned to paint next. Her suspicion was palpable. She dropped hint after hint at the damage he would cause if he painted José. Frustrated more so by the precious time she kept taking from him than by her indirect urgings to do things her way, Francisco responded, "I'm going to paint José, and I don't care what you have to say about it. He was, he *is* a student here, and he *is* in my grade, and you told me to paint *everybody* in my grade, and that's what I'm going to do."

At this the principal's eyes clenched together. Without responding, she turned and walked away. By the end of the day, Francisco had completed five more portraits, painting each one carefully and beautifully. Over the next two days, he completed twelve more portraits. He didn't attend a single class, nor did he step foot in Evil's office. All he did was paint, the days passing by like the turning of pages.

12.

It was Friday, the final day of school, and there were six portraits left to complete. Francisco gazed through the window of his father's car. The sky was clear, not a single cloud had chosen to come out, thus providing him with a calming background that suited his final day's work perfectly. When he arrived at school, just as the bell started ringing, he made his way through the building's main hallway, but stopped, when standing before him were Carlos and Ulises, glaring at him menacingly, their arms folded in front of them. Francisco looked around. There were no other students. Despite being the last day of school, they had all obediently rushed to their classes at the behest of the ringing bell."

"What do you want?" Francisco asked.

The two older, bigger boys approached him, grins spreading across their faces as they inched closer and closer. "Today is the last day for you to finish your paintings," Carlos said.

Backpedaling until he was stifled by a rusted locker, Francisco was stuck. Staring directly at the faces of the two boys, he replied, "Yes, I have six more."

"You have five more," Ulises said stepping in front of Carlos.

Francisco took a deep breath and closed his eyes. The darkness was brief, lasting only a moment, but allowed him to see the smiling face of José's sketch sitting peacefully in his mind. When Francisco opened his eyes, he responded, "I have *six* more."

Carlos laughed and nodded at Ulises who clenched his right hand into a fist, reared it back and threw it toward Francisco's midsection. Feeling the full thrust of the punch Francisco gasped, his body keeling forward.

"I think you have a problem with counting," Carlos said. "You have five more paintings to do before the final bell today. Nobody wants to see a picture of some dead kid whose face was peeled off."

Unable to stand, Francisco crashed to the floor. He looked up just in time to see Ulises rear his right foot back just as he did his fist and kick him in the ribs. Tears fell from Francisco's eyes as Carlos knelt down. "Just do what we say," he said.

Turning his head to the side, as he found Carlos' breath repulsive, Francisco replied, "No."

Carlos looked back up at Ulises, who responded with a sadistic grin and the theatrical cracking of his knuckles. Preparing for the next blow, Francisco closed his eyes and saw the sketches of the six remaining students he was determined to paint. With the exception of José's sketch, all of the sketches feverishly screamed for the chance to get out, but amidst their collective cries, there was one shouting voice that was much louder, and even more spirited. Francisco opened his eyes. The abuse he braced for never came. When he looked around, he saw the two older boys casually walking away, snickering loudly, their biting laughter bouncing off the rows of lockers, unleashing a haunting echo reverberating throughout the lengthy corridor. Confused, Francisco looked to the other side, and saw, far down the hallway, the source of the powerful voice that distinguished itself from those in his mind: Mrs. Ochoa.

He managed to stand back up, assessing the damage his body had endured and accepting that nothing was broken, nothing was permanent, and more importantly nothing was injured severe enough to hinder his ability to work. All he felt was the pain, just pain. He made his way toward Mrs. Ochoa. Her face was red, her eyes moist, deluged with concern, her mouth closed, slammed shut. She retreated into her classroom. Francisco opened the door and walked in. There she was, alone, standing in front of her desk, staring at the portrait of Evil resting on its mantle.

"Mrs. Ochoa?"

The teacher turned, looked at Francisco and asked, "Are you okay?"

He nodded, said he was, and told her it would take more than a punch, a kick and a threat to stop him from painting the six portraits he had left to complete.

The teacher forced a smile and said, "I can't wait to see them when they're finished."

Throughout the morning and the early afternoon, Francisco completed five more portraits. The school's surrounding wall, covered with the murals of students who all shared the same grade, the same blazing red eyes and the same joyous laughter had space for just one more, the one he wanted to paint most of all. José's youthful sketch was the only one left in his mind, but Francisco, who had already prepared the necessary mixtures of paint needed to release it, began to question if whether or not he *should* set it free. Though it resembled the rest of the sketches, it was unique, for it lacked the hostility found in the others. It lacked their rage, their fury, their fierce desire to express their feral vexation and their insatiable need to be freed. José's sketch seemed happy to remain where it was. *Did it really need to be freed? Wasn't it already free? Wasn't it already given all the space it could ever want? Did the sketch even need the wall anymore?* Francisco leaned against his mobile table when he heard steps approaching him from behind. He turned, and standing in front of him was Veronika. "So," she said, "did you manage to finish all of the portraits?"

He sighed, lowered his head and said no. He told her he wasn't sure if he should paint José. He left out Evil's aversion to him painting the murdered student, as well as the incident with her nephews, viewing their intimidation as irrelevant, for the true source of his doubts rested with him, and him alone. Veronika got closer until she was near enough for him to feel her breath on his face. His cheeks burned. "I know how horrible the newspaper photo was," she said, "but look how amazing the portraits are. Look how you managed to turn all of those terrible stories into all of these beautiful paintings."

His head rose. "But I don't want José to look like the rest of them," he said. "Look at their eyes, look how angry they all are. I don't want to paint him like that. Whoever killed him took away his eyes and I don't want to replace them with eyes like that. You have no idea how angry the sketches were, or how loud they screamed in my mind. They were like prisoners ready to rip the bars from their cells."

"But look at their smiles," she said. "They went through such horrible things and they're still laughing, and because of you they'll be laughing forever. That's a gift, Francisco, a gift I think José deserves, probably more than any of us."

"But he *is* smiling. He *is* laughing," Francisco replied, "in my mind, where he's safe, where he's *still* alive."

"But only you can see him there," Veronika said, "and I want to see him. We all want to see him. That's what will *really* keep him alive."

"What about his eyes?"

Veronika turned and looked at the rest of the portraits before turning back around and responding, "You've given every single one us a fire that burns against Evil, and you managed to put it in our eyes, where it will burn forever, and I think he'd want that same fire, too."

Francisco turned and stared at the vacant area where he planned to paint José. He returned his attention to Veronika and thanked her. She smiled, told him she knew he'd make the right choice and she'd see him Monday, at the assembly. After thanking her again, he watched her turn and walk away. He approached the rickety table where his arsenal lay. He closed his eyes, basked in the serenity of José's smiling sketch, opened his eyes and transferred the image to the wall. The bell rang for the last time, but its blaring was swiftly drowned out by stampeding students' celebratory chants of, *"We're free. We're free. We're free."*

With his wrist aching and sweat bubbling on his forehead, Francisco dipped the bristles of the smallest of the five brushes into the small pool of red paint and filled in one of José's eyes. He was about to fill in the second eye when he felt Evil approaching from behind. He lowered the brush, turned and there she was. The make-up on her face was thick, making her look more like a painting than the paintings occupying the wall surrounding her.

"I told you not to paint him."

"I had enough time to do it," Francisco replied, "so I did."

He took three steps away from the wall and took an additional step aside, allowing Evil to position herself directly in front of José's portrait. She complimented it, looked around and complimented all the other portraits furiously staring back at her. She turned around and faced Francisco. Armed with a smirk that made him scowl, she thanked him.

Still holding the smallest of the five brushes in his hand, he was silent. The principal stepped away from the wall and approached him. He stepped back toward the wall. When they both passed each other, Evil brushed her body against his arm, causing him to grip the brush in his hand even tighter. Now facing José's portrait, he raised the brush and was about to fill in the second eye, when the principal said, "I'm sorry, Francisco."

He spun around. Small drops of red paint leapt from the tips of the brush's bristles and whizzed through the air with reckless abandon, nearly striking the principal in the face.

"Why?" he questioned.

"Even though you've done a great job, I still must expel you."

"*What? Why?*" he shouted. "I finished all of the portraits."

"No you didn't."

He whipped his body around, dashed to the portrait, raised his hand, and dabbed the tip of the brush against its vacant eye socket, when the principal told him to stop.

"It's too late," she said, "the bell already rung. If you would have listened to me in the first place, you would have finished all the portraits I wanted you to finish with time to spare, but you chose not to listen. You chose to disobey me."

He spun around yet again and was about to respond before Evil took a pronounced step toward him and said, "Obedience is important, Francisco, and you showed a complete disregard for it. You didn't just disrespect me, you disrespected the school."

She raised her hand, extended her index finger and tapped the long nail extending far beyond its tip against the school's crest stitched on Francisco's shirt.

"As you know, along with being expelled, the tuition your parents paid for next year will also be forfeited. You remember that word, right? In any case, since it's too late now to put the official paperwork through, I'll be filing it after the assembly on Monday, which I expect you to attend, unless you have no plans on ever attending another school in this city again, of course."

"You planned on expelling me the whole time, didn't you?" he said. "If it wasn't for this, it would have been for something else, wouldn't it? So why wait until now to tell me?"

The principal stepped toward him, extended both of her arms, pointed at as many portraits as she could, and said, "Look around you, Francisco. They're amazing, beautiful, perfect, the most life-like portraits I've ever seen. I couldn't risk having you leave school before you finished all of them, or at least nearly finished all of them. Having all of these magnificent portraits on the wall guarantees me school of the year awards for the next decade, and do you know the best part about them?"

He refused to give the principal a response.

"They're free," she said. "Do you have any idea how much I would've had to pay to have portraits of this quality painted by professionals?"

Incensed tears streamed from Francisco's eyes.

"I did everything you wanted, *everything*," he said. "When my parents find out about this, they're going to kill me."

With a pitiless smile stretched across her face, the principal replied, "Obedience and respect are hard lessons to learn."

The principal turned around, took two steps away, paused, turned back around and with her scathing grin still intact, said, "I really want to thank you again for all of your hard work, Francisco. These portraits are truly breathtaking. They look so alive it almost seems like they could reach out and touch me."

He rushed to the mobile table, and with no clear intent, no foresight as to what would happen as a result, no plan to speak of, he violently pushed it toward the principal, who, after hearing a single revolution of the table's squealing wheels, abolished her smirk and put her hands over her ears.

"What is that *awful sound*?"

She glared at the table.

"Francisco, I want you to bring that table into my office, so I can get rid of it."

Evil turned her back and walked off, leaving Francisco standing behind the table, the small brush still in hand, his tears already beginning to dry. He approached José's portrait. It appeared to be winking at him, as only half of one of its eyes was filled with red paint. He asked the portrait what to do, but there was no reply. He beseeched the portrait for answers, but received none. His dejection made way for anger that grew into rage. He screamed at the portrait, demanding to know why the innocent young boy who inspired it was dead, while the Evil responsible for his death was allowed to live. Still receiving no answers, Francisco raised his right hand and thrust the tip of the small brush against the portrait's incomplete eye. His piercing strike had such force that drops of red paint spattered back, striking the crest on his shirt. Wasting no time, he speared the brush against the eye again, but this time his strike was so fierce the brush snapped in half, leaving him with a small wooden nub. He looked down and saw the other, much larger half of the brush on the ground. He knelt down. While still holding the small piece of fractured wood in one hand, he picked up the larger piece with the other. It looked like a broken bone.

With both pieces of the brush held in each hand, he stood and approached his mobile table and gently placed both pieces on it. He turned toward José's portrait. The incomplete eye was a mess. Red paint was smeared all around it, making it look like it had suffered an injury. Filled with guilt and regret, he approached the portrait. As he got closer, the extent of the damage he inflicted grew more and more apparent. When he finally stood face to face with José's mural, he lowered his head and covered the portrait's eyes with the palms of his hands. Ashamed, his eyes grew moist. Tears formed and fell, soaking his hands down to the tips of his fingers. Standing in despair, he raised his head, pleaded with the portrait for forgiveness, raised one of his hands, extended a single finger and pressed it against the damaged eye. When no forgiving words came from the portrait, he removed his finger and jumped back when he noticed the wound had showed signs of recovery. He looked down at his fingertip and saw traces of smudged red paint. He looked back at the mural and delicately dabbed his moistened finger against José's injured eye until it was completely healed. Francisco then took a step back and smiled at the portrait. No longer caring about Evil's punishment and whatever consequences he was to suffer as a result of it, no matter how dire, all he cared about was that all the ninety-two portraits were finished.

He walked back toward his mobile table, but stopped when he heard the oddest of sounds. Though familiar, he couldn't identify exactly what it was or where it came from. He looked in every direction, but saw nothing. He turned back toward the table, and heard the same sound again. He rotated his body, and was once again left confused as there was nobody in sight. Completely silent, he stood where he was. He didn't move a muscle, listening for anything that would give away the position of the person who made the sound, but there was nothing except the portraits on the wall. He shook his head, looked down and saw the drops of red paint covering the golden crest on his shirt. He slapped his hand against the crest and wiped it, spreading the paint all over it, defaming it. He then grabbed the corners of the table, but before he could take a single step he heard the same sound as before. This time, there was no mistaking what it was: laughter, joyous and jubilant laughter. He turned around, but there was still nobody in sight. Confused, he stared at José's portrait. It stared back at him intensely, with a pair of inflamed eyes and a wide open smile.

13.

Edna Espinosa yawned. She was tired, but anxious. She couldn't wait for the sun to rise and introduce the next day, when she'd be accepting her sixth straight school-of-the-year award. Wearing a pair of custom-made pajamas underneath an expensive silk robe comfortably encasing her body, she rose from a brand new, emerald green chair she had imported from Europe. Framed with the finest wood, adorned with the softest cloth, it was a magnificent example of prodigious craftsmanship. She approached the front door of her spacious home and flicked off a series of light switches, darkening her abode. She walked through her living room. Guided by memory, she didn't bump into a single thing. Halfway through the room, she stopped, approached the balcony, opened a large glass door and passed through the doorway. The air was crisp and gusty, but the spring season tempered any semblance of cold. She gazed at the moon. It wasn't totally full, but substantial enough to shimmer in the darkness of the night sky. She approached the balcony's freshly lacquered, wooden railing. She leaned against it and peered down. Her home, buoyed by a series of large, powerful stilts, overlooked the city like a castle. She took a deep breath, sucking in the cool air she believed was fresher, better than the stifling, polluted air inhaled by those residing in the city down beneath her.

She remained on the balcony, shifting her vision from the moon above and the masses below, secure at how firmly settled between the two she was, when she heard a series of loud bangs from inside the house. She went into the kitchen and felt the same persistent breeze she did on her balcony. She looked at the window above the sink. It was open. The moonlight shined upon her finely tiled floor, illuminating several jagged shards of what was once a set of colorful *Murano* glass champagne flutes she'd left on the countertop.

She considered cleaning up the mess, but thought better of it, knowing her maid would be there to clean it up in the morning. She went to the opened window, closed it, stepped around the shattered flutes, approached the refrigerator, opened its stainless steel door, grabbed a single, long stemmed cherry from a spotless glass bowl, ate it and stepped away. Before hearing the refrigerator door close, she took two steps, but seethed in pain when a large piece of glass the moonlight failed to reveal pierced through the skin on the bottom of her foot. She attempted to walk, but stopped when the throbbing in her foot stunted her movements, hindering them severely. She gingerly raised her foot, drops of blood pouring down into a hideous red footprint.

Putting all of her weight on her good foot, she limped toward a drawer inside the kitchen, careful to avoid the other shards of glass littering the floor, the blood following her obsessively. She opened the drawer, grabbed a white towel and wrapped it tightly around her gored foot. It was only a matter of seconds before a large red stain formed in the center of the cloth. Still limping, she grabbed a broom from a crevice between the wall and the refrigerator and clumsily swept up the pieces of broken glass. She eventually formed a pile of debris that she swept aside to a corner of the kitchen floor. She turned and gazed at the burgundy trail following her every step. Disgusted at the sight, she turned off the light and left the kitchen.

Her mind focused on her injured foot, which, despite the makeshift dressing she applied to it, continued to bleed. She went into the larger of the two luxurious washrooms inside her sprawling home. Once inside, she flicked on the light, the room was enormous, the ceiling high, the floor glistened, and the odor was pleasant and arousing. Sitting in the center of the majestic washroom was a vanilla marble Jacuzzi large enough to swallow her whole. She turned on both gleaming, gold faucets and watched the water pour down, filling the massive tub with hot water, a mist of steam hovering over its rising surface.

She sat on a nearby stool, removed the blood-soaked towel from her injured foot and tossed it into the washroom's matching, vanilla marble sink, knowing her maid would take care of it the next day, too. She grabbed a second towel and pressed it against the wound, trying to slow the flow of blood. With the tub already half-full, she removed the second towel, tossed it into the sink and dipped her feet into the water. Red plumes puffed out from the gash in her foot.

She removed her silk robe, followed by her pajamas and undergarments, and tossed them to the floor, exposing her naked body. Aged and frail, her flaccid breasts sagged, her gut protruded, and her legs, full of varicose veins, wobbled. When she contorted herself in an effort to scale the tubs walls, creases seen throughout her body opened up like cracks in barren soil. After stepping into the water, she positioned her body in the center of the tub and submerged herself, allowing the balmy water to soak her hair and wash away whatever make-up was left on her face. After sitting in the tub for thirty minutes, she took several deep breaths, wiping away beads of sweat bubbling from her forehead. Feeling dizzy from the heat, she rose, the water rippling and cresting, creating bloody waves that crashed against the tub's walls.

Slowly she eased her body out of the gaping tub, stepped out and planted her injured foot on the ground. It had stopped bleeding for the moment, but still seared with pain. Nude and dripping wet, she grabbed a large towel, dried off her pruning figure then dried her hair. Cleansed of the coloring chemicals that blessed it with artificial life, the rich maroon color of her hair was gone, leaving behind a matted field of grey strands that thinned out near the center of her scalp, revealing a small bald spot. Afterwards, she put on her undergarments and pajamas, and once again encased herself within the security of her silk robe.

Still feeling dizzy, she lurched her way out of the washroom. With the darkness of her home permeating throughout, she made her way to her bedroom, limped inside and turned on the light. In front of her was an extravagant King size bed topped with exquisite, pure white, Egyptian cotton sheets. Flanked by custom-made dressers, shelves and a bedside table topped with an ornately designed porcelain lamp, she looked around at several pictures hanging on the wall, capturing her relationships with various members of the city's upper crust. One picture in particular, a large framed photo of her embracing one of the nation's most popular soccer players, brought back blissful memories of a magnificent time with him after a party where every glass was full and every grin was grand. She turned off the light.

She approached her bed that was large enough to fit her five times over, took off her silk robe and hung it on a nearby hook. She jumped on the bed, rolled three times before settling in the center and buried herself underneath the soft white sheets. With her head resting comfortably against one of her many lavish pillows, she looked at the wall across from her and gazed at a large self-portrait staring back at her, smiling approvingly. She closed her eyes and envisioned herself reading the acceptance speech she had prepared for the assembly scheduled to begin at one o'clock the next morning.

Standing behind a podium set in the center of a stage high above a crowd of students, parents and teachers, she was midway through her speech when she paused to glance at the spectators, all gazing at her with adoration, and offered them a magnanimous smile. With the spotlight shining on her, and her alone, she re-commenced her speech, speaking loudly into the microphone's chrome top, but was interrupted by an impertinent, seditious sound. It was the sound of disrespect, the sound of mockery, the sound of laughter.

She opened her eyes and standing in front of her enormous bed was a girl with thick black hair, a school uniform with an all too familiar golden crest stitched on the shirt, and a pair of bright red, fiery eyes.

"What the hell are you doing in my house?"

The girl remained silent. A smile spread across her face.

"I suggest you answer me right now or else… wait, I know who you are, you're… it doesn't matter what your name is, but you have a lot of nerve coming into my home.

The girl turned and walked away, leaving Ms. Espinosa alone with nothing but the sound of her own voice. She rolled three times before reaching the edge of her bed, swung her legs and tumbled off. Her injured foot was the first to touch the spotless floor, causing a rush of pain to surge throughout her body. Wincing, she stood carefully. Putting most of the weight on her good foot, she grabbed her silk robe, wrapped it around her body, moved as fast as her in-jured foot would permit, turned on the light and exited her room. Standing just outside her bedroom door, she saw no trace of the girl. The house remained dark, except for a small crescent of light extending out of the bedroom's doorway.

"Where are you?" she said. "I know you're in here. When I find you, I'm going to—"

She heard laughter from a far corner of the cavernous living room and another round of laugher from another corner. Realiz-ing the girl must not be alone, she took a step back. The laughter blared out again, much louder than before, this time from all sides of the room, as if it were coming from the walls themselves. She spun around on her good foot, but couldn't see anything. Just as she was about to demand those responsible for the laughter show themselves, the laughter ceased. She reached for a nearby light switch and flicked it on.

Standing before her was an army of adolescence, all wearing the same school uniforms with the same golden crests stitched on their shirts, all staring at her with the same scorching eyes. Emerging from the horde of students, the same girl, whose name Ms. Espinosa still couldn't recall, stepped forward until she was within striking distance. Unsure of what the girl was going to do, Ms. Espinosa took another step back, re-entering her bedroom. The pressure of the stride against her injured foot was agonizing, but she refused to show the students an iota of weakness.

"What are you going to do?" she questioned. "What are *any* of you going to do?

None of the students replied.

"You're *all* going to be expelled! Do you hear me? *All* of the fees your parents paid for next year are going to be *forfeited*. And unless all of you get out of my home right now, I'll make sure none of you get into any school in the city. I will gladly see to it that *none* of you see the inside of a classroom again!"

The girl laughed in Ms. Espinosa's face. Enraged by the student's audacity, Ms. Espinosa stared into the girl's blazing red eyes and viciously berated her, scolding her with the same vitriol that sent countless students, countless times before, cowering away, their bodies shaking, their eyes dampened with tears, but at this moment, on this night, her efforts were futile, for the girl didn't respond with fear, but with even more laughter.

Maddened by the girl's unflappable mirth, Ms. Espinosa opened her hand, raised it, reared it back and swung it as hard as she could. Strong and fierce, the slap was right on target, but instead of feeling the impact of her palm against the young girl's face, all she felt was the weightless resistance of empty air. She reared her hand back and swung it again, and again, and every time she was met with the same empty result. She took another step back, drawing her further into the confines of her beautiful bedroom. The smiling girl took a step toward her, while the students behind her, all armed with joyful grins, remained deathly quiet.

"Do you think I'm actually *afraid* of any of you?" Ms. Espinosa shouted.

She clenched her fists, but cringed, as her long nails pierced her skin before snapping, one by one, falling to the floor with feeble clicks. She opened her hands and looked down. Blood poured out from four punctures on each palm and splashed to the floor. She looked back up and overheated with rage when she saw the girl's smile, as well as the smiles on the rest of the students' faces, grow larger. She thrust both of her injured hands forward. With her talon-less fingers outstretched, she attempted to wrap them around the young girl's throat. She hoped to feel the girl's soft skin contracting in her bloody grasp, but all she could feel were the fresh wounds in her palms. She desperately wished to hear the girl's cries for mercy, but the only sound she heard was the disturbance of vacant air.

The girl's smile remained steadfast as she took another step toward Ms. Espinosa, who responded with yet another retreating step of her own. Now in the center of her bedroom, she looked around, hoping to see something that could be of assistance. Spotting her porcelain lamp, she turned her back to the girl, rushed over and grabbed it with both hands, but as she raised it, drops of blood rained down on her from her pierced palms, splashing her face, before entering her eyes, temporarily blinding her. With her eyes sealed and stinging, the lamp slipped out of her lubricated clench. Smashing against her uninjured foot, the lamp broke into several large, jagged chunks, one of which cut her deeply, causing even more of her blood to spill. The pain was excruciating, not only matching, but surpassing the agony felt in her foot. It took all of her strength to keep from collapsing and clenching her body into a fetal position.

Students filled her bedroom, closing in on her. The air grew thinner. She wiped the blood from her eyes. Stifled, she watched the students look around as if they were inside a museum, a gallery, a palace. One student, a boy, tall and athletic, whose name she could not recall, focused on the picture hanging on the wall capturing the embrace between her and the famous soccer player. The man who shared the photo with her publicly stated on numerous occasions the importance of cultivating school athletics on a national scale, a sentiment she publicly agreed with whenever a flock of cameras focused on her. The boy raised his hands to the large, glass-faced, finely framed photo, but before he could touch it, she shouted, "*Stop*, leave it alone. *Get away from it.*"

The boy turned to her and smiled, his eyes burning red. Stirred by the boy's impudence, she rushed to him, but he refused to step away from the large photo. She outstretched her ravaged hands, anticipating the chance to grab the boy and tear him away from one of her most cherished memories, but when she reached him, her hands passed right through him, and instead of striking the boy as she had hoped they collided with the photo, causing it to fall off the wall and strike the floor with a crash. She knelt down, turned the photo over and gasped. It was cracked, disfiguring both the faces of her and the athlete standing next to her. When she looked up, the athletic boy gazed back at her. His mouth opened in a wide smile before boisterous laugher started blasting out.

She stood. A small pool of blood surrounded her. Her feet throbbed. Her hands burned. She took a step and stopped after being struck by a blow of dizziness. She shook her head, doing her best to clear the fog clouding her mind. The students scattered throughout Ms. Espinosa's bountiful bedroom, their joyous laughter heard throughout. She looked at her bed and saw four students comfortably lying on her pale sheets, side by side, with room to spare. Appalled, she limped toward them, leaving a trail of bloody footprints behind. She raised both of her hands and slapped them down on the bed, hoping it would ward off the students as if they were annoying flies. Instead, both of her palms plunged onto the sheets, staining them with bloody handprints, while the students remained where they were, staring directly at her, laughing loudly. In a fit of rage, she slapped her hands down again and again, and each time her palms struck, soaking and soiling the sheets, reducing them to a set of worthless rags.

Then there were a series of bangs coming from the kitchen. With the fog in her head growing thicker, she left the bedroom and made her way to the kitchen, once again leaving behind a trail of bloody footprints. When she reached the kitchen, she turned on the light. There was a boy, tall and gangly, dressed in the same school uniform as the other students. Standing stiffly in front of her large, opened, stainless steel refrigerator, the frail boy didn't touch anything inside. He just stood there, staring at the contents. When she got closer, the boy turned and stared at her, his eyes ablaze. She took three steps closer to him. He didn't move. She glanced into her refrigerator. It was packed with food, from fruits and vegetables, to pies and cakes, to soda and juice, all patiently waiting to be prepared for her whenever she wanted by her maid. None of those contents appeared to be the primary focus of the boy however. Instead, his attention rested on the refrigerator's center shelf, where a pre-cooked whole chicken secured within a thin layer of cellophane wrap rested on a large plate.

"What are you doing?" she said. "Did you want to eat all of my food, too? Is that it? You and all your friends want to destroy my house *and* eat my food?"

The boy turned to her and flashed an all too familiar grin.

"Wait a minute," she said after taking a step back, while clenching her fists, aggravating the wounds in her palms, causing more drops of blood to escape her body. "You did something to that chicken, *didn't you?* That's why you're standing there, that's why you're staring at it. That was your plan, *wasn't it?*"

The boy remained silent and returned his gaze to the large, cellophane wrapped poultry. In a fit of anger, she lunged in front of the boy and grabbed the plate holding the chicken. The boy stepped aside. Holding the plate in her bloodied hands, she glared at the boy. He responded with the same smile as the other students. With her anger intensifying by the second, she balanced the large plate in one hand, while tearing the wrapping off the chicken with the other. The boy continued staring at her silently, his smile undeterred.

"I know you did something to this chicken," she said after tossing the cellophane wrap to the floor, "but I'll be damned if you, or any of your friends prevent me from enjoying what's mine."

She grabbed a mammoth chunk of the cold chicken and savagely tore it off with her bloody fingers, soaking the chunk with her own blood in the process.

"You see that," she said, "this is better than any of the food you're ever going to eat."

She took a rapacious bite, followed by another and another, until her mouth was full. Her cheeks inflated. Stringy pieces of gristle leaked out of the corners of her smacking lips. She smiled as she chewed. The boy smiled back. Her smile vanished. The chicken's initial flavor made way for a metallic taste that made her violently heave, but with her mouth teeming with the blood-soaked meat she so gluttonously shoveled in, relief was impossible. Desperate for an escape from the revolting taste, she frantically looked around, but all she could see was the boy staring at her, smiling. With the nauseating tickle in her stomach warning her of what was to come, the plate she held in her other hand wobbled before tumbling out of her grasp and smashing on the floor, destroying what was left of the chicken. She leaned forward, heaved and vomited.

"You *poisoned* me." she said.

She rushed to the refrigerator, leaned her body inside, grabbed every piece of food, every glass bottle, every plastic container and tossed it all behind her. Bottles shattered, dishes smashed, containers cracked and every kind of food, from avocados and her bowl of long-stemmed cherries to bread and a block of aged cheddar cheese, was flung from the refrigerator's interior, discarded and dismissed. With the refrigerator completely empty, she shuffled toward her cupboards, kicking aside whatever items of food were in her way. She tossed everything inside the cupboard to the floor with a sweep of her forearm. Cans smacked against the floor and dented, while jars crashed and exploded. There wasn't a single spec of flooring that wasn't covered in food, plastic, liquid, glass or tin. Weak, exhausted, sweating, with her head feeling lighter and the dizziness getting worse, she stared at the boy. Amidst several deep breaths, she told him, with the sickening taste of her own blood and vomit resonating along the surface of her tongue and roof of her mouth, that he could never beat her, that she'd won.

The boy's mouth opened. Laughter spilled out. Before she could respond with all of the rage churning within her empty gut, the boy turned his back and walked away. She took a step in pursuit, but stopped and shrieked in pain when she stepped on one of the small shards of glass littering the floor, reopening the wound on the bottom of the foot she injured earlier. With the tension in her body stiffening her joints, the contracting motion of leaning down while raising her gored foot was agonizing. She pulled the piece of glass out, and as if she pulled the cork out of a titled bottle of red wine, blood poured out of the wound and splashed on the floor. She grabbed a nearby dishtowel, and just as she did before she wrapped it tightly around her foot, staving the flow. She left the kitchen. The infestation of youth now plagued the entirety of her home. Seeking refuge, she approached the emerald green chair in her living room, but froze when she spotted a chubby female student sitting on it.

"What are you doing in my chair?"

The girl looked up. Her eyes shared the same furious color as the other students.

"Get out of my chair," Ms. Espinosa said.

The girl responded with a smile that made Ms. Espinosa's entire body twitch. Her hands compressed in an unbreakable clench that turned every single one of her knuckles white, blood leaking out of her fists. She rushed to her prized chair, where the girl remained seated, and slammed her fists down, hoping to pulverize the student into submission, but the only thing her fists pummeled was the chair's plush material. After a few moments of concentrated abuse, the chair was covered in blood beaten so brutally into its weakened hide that it was destined for nowhere else but the garbage. Fatigued from the fruitless assault, she stood, turned and watched the girl walk away, hearing her laughter grow louder and louder. Out of breath, with the weight of her head getting lighter, and the spinning of the room getting more intense, Ms. Espinosa searched for the nearest wall, opened her hands, placed her palms flat against the surface and leaned against it. She inhaled deep, stood straight, removed her hands from the wall and stared at two red handprints staring right back at her. Repulsed, she took four stammered steps back and nearly tripped on a small ottoman she forgot was there, but regained her balance by grabbing hold of a small table. When she turned and released her grip from the table, she saw another set of bloody handprints gazing back at her.

She spun around, causing the cloth wrapped around her foot to shift, exposing the fresh wound, allowing even more blood to spill. She slipped on the small pool of blood, stretching it into a fiendish grin. Crumbling to the ground, she thrust both of her opened hands forward and broke the fall. Raising her hands, leaving behind a pair of bloody handprints, she leaned back, stood and took a step back. To her horror, she saw a hideous face with exploding eyes smiling at her from the floor. She turned and limped toward her bedroom. Stretched out bloody footprints followed her. She no longer felt like she was walking, but floating. Everything around her was blurred. Once inside the room, she stared at the crowd of students who continued playing, blissfully ignoring her. With the dizziness making way for an insatiable need to sleep, she shuffled toward the bed. It was left vacant. Fading fast, she moved to the side of her bed, closed her eyes, wrapped her arms around herself and let her body collapse. She rolled three times until she was in the center of the bed. She stared straight ahead, but instead of seeing the comforting sight of her own smiling, self-portrait, she saw a shirtless boy, whose neck, chest, arms and wrists were covered in sallow bruises. There was no golden crest on the boy's battered, bare chest, but she knew he was a student of hers. She nervously swallowed and gagged at the lingering taste of her own poison, and turned her attention back to the boy, his eyes aflame.

The boy approached, his hands balled into fists. Within arm's reach, he flung one fist forward, striking her in the eye, but before she could react, he flung the other fist forward, striking her in the other eye. She could feel both eyes swelling, closing shut, but not fast enough to prevent her from seeing the boy step back, his small, slim eyes smoldering, a smile spread across his face, laughter roaring out of his mouth. She grabbed her soiled sheets with both hands, pulled them up and over her face and closed her eyes.

Back at the podium in the school's airy auditorium, she stood triumphantly. There was no pain, not a mark seen or felt on her hands, feet or face. An entire crowd of people, their faces obliterated by the spotlight focused solely on her, awaited the rest of her acceptance speech that was so rudely interrupted by a belligerent few. She opened her mouth, anxious to celebrate her glory with every proceeding word, but instead of reciting her speech the only word she was able to say was *Evil*. She closed her mouth, regrouped and tried to speak again, but just as before, the only word permitted to escape her mouth was *Evil*. She tried again, and again, and every single time the result remained the same: *Evil, Evil, Evil, Evil.* What terrified her most however, was the voice uttering the single chilling word was not her own, but that of somebody else, somebody much younger.

Her bludgeoned eyes opened. She lowered her sheets. Sitting at the foot of the bed was a handsome boy. He was younger than the rest of the students occupying her bedroom. He leaned forward and smiled. Unable to speak, she stared at the boy's face. His eyes differed from the other students. They weren't red and scorching, but colorless and empty, as if they weren't even there. Her view shifted when the boy gazed downward. Her eyes widened when she saw several handprints of smeared blood muddled all over her sheets. She tossed the fouled coverlets aside and screamed when she saw the same bloodstains all over her silk robe, swathing her in a macabre embrace. She sat up and tore the robe off her body and flung it away. She looked back at the boy whose vacant eyes fixated solely on her, just like the spotlight in her dream.

Wearing only her pajamas, she lay back down. The boy closed in on her. She summoned the last bit of bitter umbrage she could and spit at the smiling boy's face, but the projected saliva flew through the boy and hit absolutely nothing. The boy's smile widened. She stared in dread when he raised his arm, brandishing one of her own large steak knives. He brought the knife down. The serrated edge of the blade sliced her face. She could feel her skin tear. The student thrust the blade down again, and again, over and over, carving her face, slashing it maniacally while laughing hysterically the entire time. Fearing the young boy, Ms. Espinosa clamped her eyes shut and turned her head from side to side, hoping it would spare her face further damage, hoping it would dissuade the student from continuing his assault, hoping there would be something left of her face when it was all over.

The boy stopped, but it did not provide her with relief, only further torture. Each abrasion hurt with its own unique, distinct potency. She was about to cry, hoping it would somehow diminish the agony of her injuries, but as the tears spilled from her swollen eyes, the salt within every droplet intensified the anguish of each wound, making her wince and whimper. She wiped the stinging tears away with the back of her hand and noticed the same girl with the head full of thick black hair she saw earlier. She was standing idly by, her arms crossed in front of her.

Unable to bear the sight of the girl and her indifference, Ms. Espinosa turned her head and saw the face of the young boy, the steak knife still held tightly in his hand, blood dripping from its teeth. The boy's eyes, no longer absent, were filled with sweltering rage. The boy's face was now close enough to feel his breath, but there was no breath to be felt. He was fearlessly inanimate, blessed with an inability to feel pity, to feel pain, to comprehend consequence. He was lifeless. But the boy was not dead, far from it, for he, like the students who continued playing and laughing in the enormous bedroom, the students she now recognized as those released upon the wall surrounding her school, were very much alive. Expecting the worst, she squeezed her eyes shut, refusing to catch a glimpse of her fate and the childish faces controlling it, and then there was nothing, no pain, no dreams, just complete, absolute darkness.

14.

Ms. Espinosa woke up. She surveyed her surroundings through rapidly moving eyes.

It was a dream, she thought, a *nightmare.*

She rolled to one side of her bed and gasped. Staring back at her were several dried-up, bloody handprints. She raised her hand and saw crusted traces of blood all over her pierced palm. She raised her other hand and saw the same thing. Breathing rapidly, she sat up, looked down and saw the same traces of dried blood surrounding her feet. She looked beyond the bed and saw her bloodied silk robe and bloodied sheets spread out on the floor. She reluctantly rolled three times on her despoiled bed, swung her legs around and carefully placed both her feet on the floor. They throbbed as soon as they made contact. Standing up, she looked around at the destruction caused by the students the night before, from the shattered lamp to the disfigured picture of her and the famous soccer player. She took two painful steps and stopped when she saw her bedroom door opening. She retreated back to her bed, but stopped when she heard a familiar voice.

"Ms, Ms, are you okay? I was so worried. I saw all the blood. I saw the mess in the kitchen. I saw your favorite chair in the living room."

Ms. Espinosa opened her eyes and faced the opening door. "I was attacked," she said, "by a group of bitches and bastards, for no reason."

"Oh my God," the maid said, opening the door completely, "your face. Are you okay?"

"You saw footprints and handprints, right? They were everywhere, *right*?"

The maid nodded.

"I did see footprints, Ms, many footprints, handprints, too, and they were everywhere, the walls, the furniture, the floor, but they all looked like they came from the same person."

The maid looked at the robe, the sheets on the floor and the stains on Ms. Espinosa's bed. Ms. Espinosa turned toward the bed then looked back at the maid. "You actually think *I* did all of this?" she said. "I should fire you for even considering that. I should put you out on the street for thinking such a thing."

The maid's head lowered and shook. "I'm sorry, Ms," she said. "No, no, it couldn't have been you. Somebody else had to be here—"

"Not just somebody else," Ms. Espinosa responded. "I told you, there was a group of them, but I'll get them back, I'll see to it they're all punished."

"I'm just happy you're safe," the maid said. "I will clean all of this up for you."

Ms. Espinosa lumbered past the maid. After passing through the bedroom's doorway, she turned and shouted, "What time is it?"

"It is almost eight-thirty, Ms."

Ms. Espinosa entered the smaller of her two washrooms. She gazed into the mirror and saw the gashes on her face. They weren't as deep as she expected them to be. Her eyes however were still swollen from the torment she endured the night before, saddled with drooping black bags. Left with no time to color her hair in the same rich, maroon shade she deemed appropriate for public consumption, she forcibly brushed the tangled grey strands atop her head and tightly tied them back in a bun. She applied heaps of foundation all over her face, covering the scars and the blackness of her bloated eyes, then brushed her teeth in an attempt to extinguish the still lingering taste of her own bile and blood. She smiled, and while the muscle action required to do so hurt immensely, she took solace in the masked reflection grinning back at her proudly. After leaving the washroom, she returned to her bedroom, where the maid was feverishly cleaning up. Smaller than Ms. Espinosa, with a much darker skin tone and tarnished uniform, the maid's appearance was further diminished as she was on her hands and knees, picking up the pieces of the previous night's mayhem. Failing to notice the woman, Ms. Espinosa bumped into her and knocked her over. Stumbling, she turned around, ignored the pain seething from her feet and scolded the maid for being in the way. The servant collected herself, got back on her hands and knees and apologized.

Ms. Espinosa shook her head, turned back around and picked out an outfit worthy of the pending celebration of her success. She ordered the maid to leave the bedroom while she changed. Without saying a word, the maid stood, slowly, her knees creaking as she vacated the bedroom. Ms. Espinosa removed her pajamas and changed into an affluent ruby red blouse and skirt, along with a pair of matching high heels that augmented the ache in her beleaguered feet, and a gold colored silk head scarf that concealed her frail, grayed hair.

She walked out of the bedroom, passed the maid without saying a word and avoided contact with any of the destruction she assumed would be cleaned up before she returned home. When she opened the front door and passed through the doorway, just before closing the door behind her she heard the maid shout from the bedroom, "Good luck, Ms."

Sitting in the driver's seat of her freshly waxed, enormous black truck, Ms. Espinosa revved the engine, shifted to reverse, backed out of her massive garage, spun the steering wheel around, shifted to drive and slammed her ailing right foot on the gas pedal. The truck raced out of her driveway with a vindictive roar.

The assembly was scheduled to start in ten minutes, and with the city's suffocating traffic as much a guarantee as the sun's rising, there was no way she would reach the school on time. At best, she would be ten, probably fifteen, most likely twenty minutes late. She nonetheless drove leisurely, inching closer and closer to the school, glancing through her window at the insignificant cars beside her, knowing the assembly would not actually start until she arrived. Along the way she looked at her rear view mirror, her veiled reflection smiling back at her as the thought of being able to exact revenge on the children who tormented her was just minutes away from becoming a reality. While debating whose expulsion form she would draft and sign first, despite the pain it caused, her grin grew wider. Elation overcame her, distracting her to the point of momentarily losing focus on driving, causing her to swerve, almost knocking a smaller car into one of the treacherous lanes of opposing traffic.

The most obvious choice to be first on the chopping block was the young boy who slashed her face, but she didn't yet know who he was. He looked just like the final portrait painted on the school's wall, but he couldn't be that student. That student was dead. Unsure if the knife wielding boy was even a student of hers at all, she put him aside in favor of those she *knew* were students of hers, starting with the girl with the thick black hair. She no longer regretted forgetting the girl's name. She would attain it soon enough, hopefully in front of her unsuspecting parents, whom she would happily inform their daughter would never again set foot in another school within the city's limits, and the tuition they paid for the next year would be forfeited. It was a marvelous thought. She vividly recalled the scrawny student who poisoned her chicken and forced her to rid her kitchen of all her food, and the chubby girl who ruined her favorite chair, and the athletic boy who destroyed one of her prized pictures, and envisioned signing the freshly printed forms that would summarily expel them all. She hoped a signed expulsion form for the shirtless boy who struck her in the face would bring him additional bruises and further grief. But, as much as the thought of expelling all of those students, along with every other student who had the audacity to torment and laugh at her, brought her joy, the one student, the one form she couldn't wait to see was the already signed piece of paper anxiously awaiting her on the corner of her desk. It already had a name written on it, a name she remembered clearly, a name she couldn't wait to destroy, the painter of her pain: Francisco Roberto Morelos. She swerved again.

She pulled into the school's parking lot. She drove by every one of the teachers' cars all obediently parked side by side in the spots she personally allocated for them. Concluding her journey, Ms. Espinosa pulled her truck into her own parking spot, the one closest to the school. She turned off the ignition, silencing the engine's growl, stepped out of the vehicle and without bothering to lock the door she made her way into the school.

She walked down the main hallway until she reached the auditorium. When she walked in, she was met with the synchronized turning of many heads. She looked beyond the audience and glared directly at the vacant podium and the chrome microphone resting in the center of it. To the side of the podium was a man in a jet black suit and bright red tie, the same man who told her three weeks prior she was a shoo-in to win the award he was set to present her in a few short moments. No applause, just stares greeted her as she approached the stage. The man glared down at her, a crooked smile smeared halfway across his face. She scaled a short staircase before stepping foot on the stage. She walked toward the man, and when she reached him he handed her the award, a gleaming, golden plaque fastened atop a block of wood. It was heavy, much heavier than it looked, much heavier than the five identical looking awards she had hanging on one of the walls in her office.

She placed the award on a small cleft at the top of the podium, turned and spread out her arms. The man did the same. The embrace was light and feathered, with both her and the refined man tapping each other's shoulders briskly, each doing all they could to not touch the other any more than they had to. After the embrace concluded, the man stood in front of the podium, grabbed the microphone and tilted it upwards, aligning it with his stature. A spotlight focused on him, illuminating his prim figure and esteemed features.

"Today I would like to introduce a great woman," he said, "a woman who has always kept the education, the welfare, the future, the *lives* of her students in the center of her heart." The man outstretched his arms and pointed at the first twenty-five rows of spectators, occupied by all of her students. "This woman has done so much over the last five years I could spend hours upon hours telling you story after story. So, it is only fitting she continued that trend of tireless effort into her sixth year, and for that I'm proud to present this award to the principal who best exemplifies what it means to run a school I can personally label this fine city's *school-of-the-year*. For an unprecedented sixth year in a row, ladies and gentlemen, I present to you Ms. Edna Espinosa."

The man clapped his hands. The rest of the crowd, with the exception of all the students seated in the first twenty-five rows, clapped right along with him. The collective applause boomed throughout the auditorium in an explosion of veneration. After the man stepped aside, Ms. Espinosa stood in front of the podium, looked up, reached for the microphone and clasped its gleaming metal shaft in her hand. Stiff as it was, the microphone proved difficult to adjust. She jiggled and fondled it, but still it wouldn't budge. Squeezing it tighter, causing a surge of pain to shoot through her body, as the punctures in her palms seized, she was finally able to relax it. With a screech, she tilted the microphone down, bringing the chrome top to her level. She opened her mouth. The spotlight, far removed from the man in the suit who now stood at the far side of the stage, focused squarely on her. She was unable to make out a single face in the crowd. All she could see was the bright light.

"Ladies and gentlemen," she said. "I would first like to say thank-you. Thank you all for allowing me to do what needed to be done to warrant this wonderful award, and to make this school a symbol from which all schools should strive to be. It requires a great deal of hard work to take a school and make it the city's best, but I want you all to know I made sure only the best interests of the school were served every step of the way."

She took a deep, relaxed breath.

"I would especially like to thank all of my students for—"

The microphone suddenly unleashed a deafening squeal. She took a step back. Her face twisted at the dreadful noise. She slammed her hands against her ears in an effort to silence the torturous sound. Outside of the spotlight's blinding gaze, she focused on the students seated in the first five rows, and in an instant the sweetness of the revenge she intended to carry out at the conclusion of the assembly soured. Gazing at her with blazing red eyes, she recognized every single one of the students as those who terrorized her the night before. She turned away, took several rapid breaths and turned back toward the microphone.

"As I was saying," she said in a cracked voice, "I would like to thank my students for—"

The microphone squealed again, louder than before. She stammered back, once again removing her from the spotlight's glare. Her eyes shifted downward and once again focused on the students. While their eyes continued to glow fiercely red, they also had smiles etched on their adolescent faces. A moment later those smiles opened and laughter exploded out of their mouths.

She attempted to recommence her speech. "I would like to thank my students for—"

It was too late, the students' laugher drowned out the principal, silencing her voice. She stepped away from the podium and looked around frantically. The man in the suit stared at her quizzically.

"Look at their eyes," she pleaded. *"Look at them."*

She looked at the crowd of parents and teachers hoping for assistance, but they all offered her nothing but puzzled expressions. Stepping toward the edge of the stage, she looked back down at the students in the first five rows. Her breathing grew faster as the laughing children started pointing at her, their hands extended in a contemptuous salute. A relentless pressure squeezed her mind. She squinted and stared at the center of the first row and staring back at her was Francisco. Enraged, she pointed at him and scolded him. The student stood, as did all his peers, and with his eyes combusting with fire, he laughed at her even harder. She took two steps back, bumped into the podium, turned around, grabbed the microphone, ripped it from its cradle and returned to the edge of the stage. She shouted into the microphone's chrome head, "I run this school, not you, *me*, I run it, and I'm going to destroy *you*. I'm going to destroy *all of you* with nothing more than a signature."

The students remained standing, pointing, laughing in her face, fueling her indignation. She raised and waved her arm from side to side, condemning the students, but as she lowered it, the tip of her longest finger caught the dangling tail of her flaxen silk crown and peeled it off, exposing a heap of disheveled grey hair. Possessed by her fervor, seeing nothing and nobody but the students, she continued, "Do you think I actually care about any of you? Do you think I care about your worthless parents? Do you think I care about these useless teachers? I don't care about any of them. I do what I want here. I've made so much money here I couldn't hope to spend it in *three-hundred lifetimes.* Do you think that little stunt you pulled last night means anything? Do you think it will change anything? Do you have any idea who I am, and what I can do? I'm—"

She abruptly ceased her shouting when she noticed Francisco utter a single word she wasn't able to hear, but was able to read on his smiling lips.

Evil.

She exhaled as the pressure pounding her skull subsided. Looking around however, an onset of panic caused her to sweat profusely. It was no longer just the eyes of the students that boiled and flamed, but also the eyes of those whose presence she overlooked in the midst of her madness: the parents and the teachers, all of whom were privy to her revelatory discourse. She took several steps back and looked at the man in the black suit and red tie. He stood by, not even bothering to look at her, reducing her to a state of anonymity.

She approached the podium and reached for the award she still firmly believed was hers, but retracted her hand at the sight of her own reflection staring back at her from the golden plaque's shimmering surface. Her hair was a dampened, ragged mess, with frail grey strands going every which way, allowing a draft to chill the exposed skin in the center of her scalp. With the last traces of foundation washed away by her sweat, the scars on her face and the blackness surrounding her dilated eyes were now fully exposed. She backed away from the award and the abominable portrait it offered her, realizing the face she saw was the same face she saw on the sketch Francisco drew of her three weeks earlier.

She kicked off her high-heeled shoes, which only further diminished her already crumbling stature, descended down the short staircase to the auditorium floor and made her way down the aisle toward the door. She glanced back at the stunned crowd who stared back at her with hate in their eyes, but had yet to manifest their fury into action. She increased her pace, but was thwarted by Ms. Vasquez, who leapt in front of her, kneeled to the ground and pledged her loyalty. Dodging the teacher without offering an acknowledgment of her presence, she continued onward, staring only at the door, her exodus, but was obstructed yet again, this time by somebody she didn't recognize, a woman, older and smaller, who appeared even more broken, more haggard than she did.

"Do you know who I am?" the woman asked.

"No," Ms. Espinosa said, "and I don't care."

"José Escutia was my grandson. I raised him after his parents died. I was hoping there would be a commemoration, a memoriam, at least a *mention* of him today, but there was nothing, not a single word, as if he never existed."

Looking around, seeing the crowd snap out of their collective spell of shock, Ms. Espinosa shoved the old woman aside and continued toward the door, but was stopped yet again, this time by Mr. Torres, who pleaded with her for an opportunity to help. Angered at the interference and anchored by adrenaline, she pushed the massive gym teacher aside, causing him to crash against a vacant chair, re-opening the inconspicuous scar on his forehead. As blood gushed from the gym teacher's skull, Ms. Espinosa looked at the crowd, who at this point started closing in on her. She turned her attention back to the door, and rushed toward it. She took no more than two steps before tripping over a foot abruptly thrust in her way. She crashed to the ground. Unable to get up as her entire body throbbed, she turned around and saw the smiling face of the person responsible for her collapse: Mrs. Ochoa.

Tearing her eyes away from the mutinous teacher, who stared back at her, laughing, Ms. Espinosa turned her attention to the awaiting door that appeared close enough to crawl to, and crawl she did, but her progress was halted by a frail hand grasping her shoulder. She turned her head. Staring down at her with a pair of searing red eyes was the same old woman who confronted her moments ago. This time however, no words were spoken. Instead, the woman flexed all five of her wrinkled fingers, cocked her hand back and brought it down in a thunderous slap that struck and ruptured Ms. Espinosa's exposed scars. In a matter of seconds, she felt more blows strike her body. The pounding was relentless as the crowd she had tried to evade had finally succumbed to the momentum and insatiable appetite of a mob.

She closed her eyes, hoping that just like the night before she could escape the assault and wake up in the comfort and security of her bed. But, when she opened her eyes, just before feeling the bottom of a boot crash against her temple, all she could see were sets of flaming red eyes and gaping smiles laughing wildly at her.

15.

Francisco watched the ferocious beating the teachers, his parents and the parents of his classmates imposed on Evil. Not caring if the principal lived or died, he realized his chance to save himself was at hand. He looked at Veronika, who stood by his side, watching Evil's comeuppance, her arms crossed in front of her.

"I have to go," he said.

Veronika didn't appear to hear him. He was going to repeat himself, but stopped, knowing it didn't matter how many times he told her he had to go. She was too enthralled by the violence, hypnotized by it, to hear him.

He made his way down the school's deserted hallway until he reached the school's main office. The office door was unlocked, and with a simple click it popped open. After taking a deep breath, he pushed the door forward. He took a step through, released his grip from the doorknob and shuddered when the door slammed shut behind him. He was alone. The atmosphere of the office was one of suspended animation, stillness and silence. He grinned. For the first time he didn't have to hear the nameless secretary's fingers pounding against the beaten keys of her keyboard. He stared at the door of Evil's chamber. It looked just as formidable as ever. He grabbed the doorknob, violently twisted it and with a click the unlocked door opened. He pushed it with both hands. The door's resistance was mighty, as was its aggressive slam once he passed through the doorway and let it go.

Inside Evil's domain, Francisco spotted the paper he sought on the corner of her desk. It sat there, comfortably, in the exact same place he'd seen it three days earlier, when he'd wheeled in his mobile table, and the principal had unleashed a malicious smile when he'd stopped and stared at the condemning sheet of paper.

"Here I am," he said. "I'm about to destroy the piece of paper you thought would destroy me."

He let out a righteous laugh, approached the desk and grabbed the form. He held it up and read it hastily. Coldly written, its conviction was finalized by Evil's signature at the bottom of the page. He tore the sheet of paper in half. Wasting no time, he put both ripped pieces on top of each other and ripped them in half. He then took the four narrow strips of paper, held them horizontally in his hands, tore each one into four small pieces, producing sixteen similarly sized dismembered squares of paper and stuffed the severed pieces deep into the depths of his pocket.

He then looked around and saw the pictures of Evil and her cohorts hugging, shaking hands, smiling, lying. He saw Evil's plaques, all five of them, suspended on one of the office's walls. He saw Evil's portrait, the same one found in every classroom within the school, perched on a smooth, wooden mantle. He turned and spotted his mobile table. He approached the table and removed the loose lid from one of the cans of paint. Staring back at him was a shallow pool of pure red. He cradled the opened can, approached Evil's desk and recklessly slammed it down, laughing as red paint jumped and splashed on the desk's black marble surface, creating a long red streak that looked like a tongue, a tail, a necktie, similar to the one he had just seen hanging from the throat of Evil's superior, the prestigious looking man in the black suit.

He walked behind the desk and shoved Evil's throne aside. His eyes widened when he spotted two drawers. He grabbed the handle of the first drawer. It was unlocked. He pulled it, and just as Mrs. Ochoa said there was a collection of identical, spotless glass-framed portraits of Evil. He pulled open the second drawer, and once again confirming his favorite teacher's words was a stack of wooden mantels. Francisco grabbed the can of red paint, swaying it back and forth, allowing even more paint to spill on Evil's desk, and poured what was left of it into each drawer, staining every mantel, defiling every portrait.

Though filled with joy, he was still faced with the unanswered question as to where he could rid himself of the pieces of paper resting at the bottom of his pocket. He scanned the confines of Evil's domain, hoping to find an appropriate final resting place for the eviscerated document, a place where its malevolent content would never be seen by anybody, ever. He spotted a door in the corner of the office, the same door he noticed three weeks earlier, but was never told what was on the other side. He tossed the empty paint can aside, caring little where it landed and what the spilled paint tarnished. He approached the door, opened his palm and grabbed the knob. Ready for something, anything, everything, he took a deep breath and opened the door. He was instantly met with an aroma so enchanting it immediately exceeded the intoxication of the air swirling throughout the interior of Evil's office. He took a single step and turned on the light. It was a washroom, Evil's private, personal washroom.

He smiled. He immediately saw the solution to his problem. His stomach grumbled. His smile grew wider. He stepped further into the illustrious washroom toward the toilet. It looked unlike any toilet he'd ever seen before. There was a small panel on one side, populated by a dozen small, multicolored buttons. The seat was padded with cushioned material. His stomach grumbled again. He approached the bizarre toilet. Standing above it, he stared into the basin's pool of still, sapphire blue water. It smelled of mint.

He unbuckled his belt, unclipped a button, unzipped the zipper of his pants, turned around, grabbed the waistband of both his pants and underwear and in a single motion, lowered them to his ankles as he lowered himself to the padded seat. There he reveled in the comfort of the toilet's plush seat. He looked down at the panel. Unsure which button he was supposed to push, he pushed them all. The panel lit up. Several different sounding beeps blared out. A second passed before he nearly jumped from the seat as he felt it getting hotter and hotter. He looked back down at the panel and read a series of small printed words written underneath the buttons he'd pounded at random.

Off.

Moderately Warm.

Warm.

Very Warm.

Hot.

Suddenly, he felt his stomach churn, and in an instant, with the heat of the soft, cushioned seat relaxing him in a way he'd never felt before, he heard a splash from the basin below. Relieving and glorious, he felt revitalized by his body's thorough, albeit rudimentary, discharge of the decay that had built up in his bowels.

He peered to his right and resting on a gleaming golden spindle was a roll of what appeared to be the thickest, softest toilet paper ever made. He reached out and playfully tugged at the dangling end piece, allowing the roll to spin rapidly until half of the paper rested listlessly on the washroom's pristine floor. He grabbed and tore off a sufficient amount of toilet paper and marveled at its softness. It was a far cry from the rugged feel of the thin toilet paper he was forced to use within the school's student washrooms, when there was any actually available. With the soft paper hand, he cleaned himself, smiling as it massaged his skin. He dropped the clump of sullied paper into the toilet. He then grabbed the waistbands of his underwear and pants, and in a single motion raised them as he raised himself from the cushioned seat. He turned around and glanced at the toilet's glistening golden lever, but he didn't pull it down.

He reached into his pocket and pulled his hand out. It was balled up in a fist. He raised it and opened it. Resting in the center of his palm were all sixteen pieces of the form detailing his expulsion and forfeiture of his parent's tuition money for the following year. He extended his hand until it rested above the foul pool below. And, with the finality of a floor disappearing beneath the feet of the fated, he rotated his hand until all of the torn pieces of paper fell into the toilet bowl. Each piece floated desperately to the surface of the water, doing all they could to not mingle with the filth floundering beneath it. He gazed at the pompous pieces of paper, smiled and pulled the toilet's shimmering gold lever. There was a loud flush. The water within the inescapable basin whirled, and the clump of soft stained toilet paper, along with Francisco's excrement, collided with the remnants of Evil's damning document, and together they were all sucked down the drain with a loud slosh.

He turned around and approached a large sink he assumed, just like the toilet, had not been used by anybody but Evil herself. The sink's faucet and handles were golden. He grabbed the gleaming handles, turned them roughly toward him and used the soap he also assumed hadn't been used by anybody but Evil herself. It was yet another luxury he was rarely afforded inside the student designated washrooms. He used it voraciously, creating a dense lather, while making no effort to avoid splashing water all over the spotless countertop. Afterwards, he turned off the water and grabbed a soft towel hanging comfortably on a golden rod. Brusquely he dried his hands, tossed the towel on the floor, turned and walked out of Evil's washroom, the sound of his laughter echoing inside, continuing on throughout her empty office and booming throughout the school's main hallway.

Acknowledgements

I would first like to thank my mother for raising me right and giving me all of the tools I needed to think for myself and write what I think. I would also like to thank Paulina Castro for sticking with me for so many years and supporting me in my work, regardless of how insufferable I can be at times. Thank you so much y te amo mucho.

I would like to thank Charlie Franco at Montag Press for giving me yet another shot with this book, which has meant a lot to me for a long time. I can't tell you enough how much it means to me to have the support you have given me, and your editing was fantastic, as it made a great story even better. I also want to thank Punto Ágora for creating an amazing cover. Muchas gracias amigo.

Finally, I would like to thank the artists I've never had the chance to meet who created a number of beautiful and heartbreaking murals throughout Mexico, from Copilco to Cancun. Your work, which shouldn't have to exist, saddened me, enraged me and inspired me to write this story as you brought so much life to the victims of Evil, and I hope I was able to carry on what you started. Muchas gracias.

Born and raised in the Scarborough area of Toronto, Canada, Jonathan R. Rose has always been surrounded by other cultures. He has constantly sought the opportunity to learn about the world from those inhabiting all parts of it. As a result, he has spent over a third of his life travelling, exploring and living in many countries, most prominently in Mexico, where has lived for nearly 10 years, and Argentina, where he lived for 2 years.

His first novel, *Carrion* was published by Montag Press in 2015. Since then he has had numerous short stories published in various online magazines, including the Spadina Literary Review, the Danforth Review and more. In addition to, *The Spirit of Laughter*, which is also published by Montag Press, in 2020 Jonathan R. Rose has also had the novel, *Gato y Lobo* published by Timón Educación in Mexico City.